STR

IVAN OSOKIN

P. D. Ouspensky was born in Moscow in 1878. His first book, *The Fourth Dimension* (1909), offered a contribution to mathematical theory; it was *Tertium Organum* (1912) and *A New Model of the Universe* (1914) which revealed his stature as a thinker and his deep preoccupation with the problems of man's existence. His meeting with Gurdjieff in 1915 marked a turning point in Ouspensky's life. From this time his interest centred on the practical study of methods for the development of consciousness in man, as expounded in *In Search of the Miraculous, The Psychology of Man's Possible Evolution* (both published after his death in 1947) and *The Fourth Way* (1957). These methods are also discussed in *A Further Record. Strange Life of Ivan Osokin*, published in 1947, the year of his death, was Ouspensky's only novel and he wrote two short stories published as *Talks with a Devil*. Arkana also publish *Conscience: The Search for Truth*, a collection of essays.

P. D. Ouspensky died in England in 1947.

P.D. OUSPENSKY

STRANGE LIFE OF IVAN OSOKIN

A NOVEL

ARKANA

ARKANA

Published by the Penguin Group
27 Wrights Lane, London W8 5TZ, England
Viking Penguin Inc., 40 West 23rd Street, New York, New York 10010, USA
Penguin Books Australia Ltd, Ringwood, Victoria, Australia
Penguin Books Canada Ltd, 2801 John Street, Markham, Ontario, Canada L3R 1B4
Penguin Books (NZ) Ltd, 182–190 Wairau Road, Auckland 10, New Zealand

Penguin Books Ltd, Registered Offices: Harmondsworth, Middlesex, England

First published in Great Britain by the Stourton Press 1947
Published by Arkana 1987
10 9 8 7 6 5 4 3 2

Copyright 1947 by P. D. Ouspensky
All rights reserved

Printed and bound in Great Britain by
Cox & Wyman Ltd, Reading

CHAPTERS

CHAPTER I
THE PARTING

ON THE SCREEN a scene at Kursk station in Moscow. A bright
April day of 1902. A group of friends, who came to see Zinaida
Krutitsky and her mother off to the Crimea, stand on the
platform by the sleeping-car. Among them Ivan Osokin, a
young man about twenty-six.

Osokin is visibly agitated although he tries not to show it.
Zinaida is talking to her brother, Michail, Osokin's friend,
a young officer in the uniform of one of the Moscow Grenadier
regiments, and two girls. Then she turns to Osokin and walks
aside with him.

"I am going to miss you very much," she says. "It's a pity
you cannot come with us. Though it seems to me that you
don't particularly want to, otherwise you would come. You
don't want to do anything for me. Your staying behind now
makes all our talks ridiculous and futile. But I am tired of
arguing with you. You must do as you like."

Ivan Osokin becomes more and more troubled, but he tries
to control himself and says with an effort:

"I can't come at present, but I shall come later, I promise
you. You cannot imagine how hard it is for me to stay here."

"No, I cannot imagine it and I don't believe it," says
Zinaida quickly. "When a man wants anything as strongly as
you say you do, he acts. I am sure you are in love with one of
your pupils here—some nice, poetical girl who studies fencing. Confess!" She laughs.

Zinaida's words and tone hurt Osokin very deeply. He
begins to speak but stops himself, then says: "You know that
is not true; you know I am all yours."

"How am I to know?" says Zinaida with a surprised air. "You are always busy. You always refuse to come and see us. You never have any time for me, and now I should so much like you to come with us. We should be together for two whole days. Just think how pleasant the journey would be!"

She throws a quick glance at Osokin.

"And afterwards, there in the Crimea, we would ride together and we would sail far out to sea. You would read me your poems—and now I shall be bored." She frowns and turns away.

Osokin tries to reply, but finding nothing to say he stands biting his lips.

"I shall come later," he repeats.

"Come when you like," says Zinaida indifferently, "but this chance is lost already. I shall be bored travelling alone. Mother is a very pleasant travelling-companion, but that is not what I want. Thank God I have seen one man I know, evidently going by this train. He may amuse me on the way."

Osokin again begins to speak but Zinaida continues:

"I'm only interested in the present. What do I care for what may happen in the future? You don't realize this. You can live in the future, I cannot."

"I understand it all," says Osokin, "and it's very hard for me. Yet I cannot help it. But will you remember what I asked you?"

"Yes, I shall remember and I'll write to you. But I don't like writing letters. Don't expect many; come soon instead. I shall wait a month for you, two months—after that I will not wait any more. Well, let us go. Mother is looking for me."

They rejoin the group by the sleeping-car.

Osokin and Zinaida's brother walk towards the station exit.

"What is the matter, Vanya?" says Michail Krutitsky. "You don't look very cheerful."

Osokin is not in a mood for talking.

"I'm all right," he says, "but I am sick of Moscow. I too should like to go away somewhere."

They come out towards the large asphalt square in front of the station. Krutitsky shakes hands with Osokin, walks down the steps, hails a carriage and drives off.

Osokin stands for a long time looking after him.

"There are times when it seems to me that I remember something," he says to himself slowly, "and others when it seems that I've forgotten something very important. I feel as though all this had happened before in the past. But when? I don't know. How strange."

Then he looks round like a man waking up.

"Now she has gone and I am here alone. Only to think I might be travelling with her at this very moment! That would be all I could wish for at present. To go south, to the sunshine, and to be with her for two whole days. Then, later on, to see her every day . . . and the sea and the mountains . . . But instead of that I stay here. And she doesn't even understand why I don't go. She doesn't realize that at the present moment I have exactly thirty kopecks in my pocket. And if she did, it would make it no easier for me."

He looks back once more at the entrance to the station hall, then with bent head goes down the steps to the square.

CHAPTER II
THE THREE LETTERS

THREE MONTHS LATER at Ivan Osokin's lodgings. A large room which is rented furnished. Rather poor surroundings. An iron bedstead with a grey blanket, a wash-stand, a chest of drawers, a small writing table, an open bookcase; on the wall, portraits of Shakespeare and Pushkin and some foils and masks.

Osokin, looking very perturbed and irritated, is walking up and down the room. He flings aside a chair that is in his way. Then he goes to the table, takes from the drawer three letters in long narrow grey envelopes, reads them one after another and puts them back.

First letter. Thank you for your letters and your verses. They are delightful. Only, I should like to know to whom they refer—not to me I am sure, otherwise you would be here.

Second letter. You still remember me? Really, it often seems to me that you write from habit or from a strange sense of duty you have invented for yourself.

Third letter. I remember everything I said. The two months are coming to an end. Don't try to justify yourself or to explain. That you have no money, I know, but I have never asked for it. There are people living here who are much poorer than you.

Osokin walks about the room, then pauses near the table and says aloud:

"And she writes no more. The last letter came a month ago. And I write to her every day."

There is a knock at the door. Osokin's friend Stoupitsyn, a young doctor, walks into the room. He shakes hands with

Osokin and sits down at the table in his overcoat.

"What is the matter with you? You're looking very ill."

He comes quickly to Osokin and with mock seriousness tries to feel his pulse. Osokin smiles and waves him away, but the next moment a shadow crosses his face.

"Everything is rotten, Volodya," he says. "I can't express it clearly to you, but I feel as though I had cut myself off from life. All you other people are moving on while I am standing still. It looks as though I had wanted to shape my life in my own way but had only succeeded in breaking it to pieces. The rest of you are going along by the ordinary ways. You have your life now and a future ahead of you. I tried to climb over all the fences and the result is that I have nothing now and nothing for the future. If only I could begin again from the beginning! I know now that I should do everything differently. I should not rebel in the same way against life and everything it offered me. I know now that one must first submit to life before one can conquer it. I have had so many chances, and so many times everything has turned in my favor. But now there is nothing left."

"You exaggerate," says Stoupitsyn. "What difference is there between you and the rest of us? Life is not particularly pleasant for anyone. But why, has anything especially disagreeable happened to you?"

"Nothing has happened to me—only I feel out of life."

There is another knock at the door. Osokin's landlord, a retired civil servant, comes in. He is slightly drunk and extremely affable and talkative, but Osokin is afraid he will ask for his rent and tries to get rid of him. When the landlord has gone, Osokin, with a look of disgust on his face, waves his hand towards the door.

"You see, the whole of life is a petty struggle with petty difficulties like that," he says. "What are you doing this evening?"

"I am going to the Samoyloffs. They are talking of forming a circle for spiritualistic, mediumistic or some such investigations—a society for psychical research in Hamovniki. Will you be there? I believe you are interested in that sort of thing?"

"Yes, I was, although I see more and more that it is all nonsense. But I am not invited. You see, I told you I had strayed from the fold. They are a set of people vaguely connected with the University, but always emphasizing this connection. What am I to them? I'm a stranger and an outsider, and it is the same everywhere. Three-quarters of their interests and three-quarters of their talk are completely foreign to me, and they all feel this. They invite me sometimes out of politeness, but day by day I feel that the gulf grows wider. People talk to me differently from the way they talk to one another. Last week three silly girl students advised to me read Karl Marx, and they did not even understand when I said I should prefer milk soup.* You see what I mean? It is certainly all nonsense, but this nonsense is beginning to tire me."

"Well, I can't argue with you," says Stoupitsyn, "but I'm sure this is all your imagination."

He gets up, pats Osokin on the shoulder, takes the book for which he came, and leaves.

Osokin also prepares to go out. Then he walks up to the table and stands there in his hat and coat, lost in thought.

"Everything would have been different," he says, "if I could have gone to the Crimea. And after all why didn't I go? I could at least have got there, and once there, what would anything have mattered? Perhaps I could have found some work. But how on earth could one live at Yalta without money? Horses, boats, cafés, tips—all that means money. And one has to dress decently. I couldn't have gone there in the same clothes I wear here. All these things are only trifles, but when these same trifles are put together . . . And she doesn't understand that I could not live there. She thinks that I don't want to come, or that something keeps me here . . . Will there really be no letter again to-day?"

* In Pushkin's *Notes* there is a story of a jester who was asked which he preferred: to be quartered or hanged. And he said he would prefer milk soup.

CHAPTER III
THE MAN IN
THE DARK BLUE OVERCOAT

IVAN OSOKIN goes to inquire whether there are any letters for him at the General Post Office where he had asked Zinaida to write to him "poste-restante." There are no letters. As he comes out, he runs into a man in a dark blue overcoat.

Osokin stops and follows the man with his eyes.

"Who is that man? Where have I seen him? The face is familiar. I know that overcoat."

Lost in thought, he walks on. At the corner of the street he stops to allow an open carriage with a pair of horses to pass him. In the carriage are a man and two ladies whom he has met at Krutitsky's house. Osokin raises his hand to take off his hat, but they do not see him. He laughs and walks on.

At the next corner he meets Zinaida's brother. The latter stops and, taking Osokin's arm, walks along with him saying:

"Have you heard the news? My sister is going to be married to Colonel Minsky. The wedding will be at Yalta, and afterwards they mean to go to Constantinople and from there to Greece. I'm going to the Crimea in a few days. Have you any message?"

Osokin laughs and shakes hands with him, and answers in a cheerful voice:

"Yes, give her my greetings and congratulations."

Krutitsky says something else, laughs and walks away.

Osokin says good-bye to him with a smiling face. But after they have parted, Osokin's face changes. He walks on for some time, then stops and stands looking down the street taking no notice of the passers-by.

"Well, so that is what it means," he says to himself. "Now

everything is clear to me. What ought I to do? Go there and challenge Minsky to a duel? But why? It was evidently all decided beforehand and I was wanted just for amusement. What a good thing I didn't go there. No, that's vile of me! I have no right to think that and it's not true. All this happened because I did not go. But I certainly shall not go now—and I won't do anything. She has chosen. What right have I to be dissatisfied? After all, what can I offer her? Could I take her to Greece?"

He walks on, then stops again and continues to talk to himself.

"But it seemed to me that she really felt something for me. And how we talked together! There was no one else in the world to whom I could talk in that way . . . She is so extraordinary! And Minsky is ordinary among the ordinary; a staff-colonel, and he reads the 'Novoe Vremya.' But quite soon he will be a man of standing—and I am not even recognized by her friends in the street.

"No, I cannot . . . I must either go somewhere or . . . I cannot stay here."

CHAPTER IV
THE END OF THE ROMANCE

EVENING. Osokin in his room. He is writing a letter to Zinaida Krutitsky, but tears up sheet after sheet and begins afresh. From time to time he jumps up and walks about the room. Then he begins to write again. At last he throws down the pen and falls back in his chair, exhausted.

"I can't write any more," he says to himself. "I have written to her for whole days and whole nights. Now I feel as though something were broken in me. If none of my other letters said anything to her, this one will say nothing. I cannot . . ."

He rises slowly and, moving like a blind man, takes a revolver and cartridges from the drawer of the table, loads the revolver and puts it in his pocket. Then he takes his hat and coat, turns out the lamp and goes out.

CHAPTER V
AT THE MAGICIAN'S

IVAN OSOKIN goes to a magician whom he has known for some time. He is a good magician, and always has excellent brandy and cigars.

Osokin and the magician sit by the fire.

A spacious room richly decorated in a half-Oriental way. The floor is covered with precious old Persian, Bokhara and Chinese carpets. High windows are curtained with ancient brocade of beautiful design. Carved ebony tables and chairs. Bronze figures of Indian gods. Indian palm-leaf books. In a recess, a graceful and almost life-size seated figure of Kwan-Yin. A large celestial globe on a red Chinese-lacquered stand. On a small carved ivory table near the magician's chair stands an hour-glass. On the back of the chair, a black Siberian cat is sitting and looking at the fire.

The magician himself, a bent old man with a sharp penetrating glance, is dressed all in black, and wears a small flat black cap on his head. He holds in his hand a thin Persian stick inlaid with turquoise.

Osokin is gloomy. He smokes a cigar and says nothing.

At the moment when he is particularly deep in thought, the magician speaks.

"My dear friend, you knew it before."

Osokin starts and looks at him.

"How do you know what I am thinking?"

"I always know what you are thinking."

Osokin bends his head.

"Yes, I know it cannot be helped *now*," he says, "But if only I could bring back a few years of this miserable time which does not even exist, as you yourself always say. If only I could get back all the chances which life offered me and which I threw away. If only I could do things differently . . ."

The old man takes the hour-glass from the table, shakes it, turns it over and watches the sand running.

"Everything can be brought back," he says, "everything. But even that will not help."

Osokin, without listening and completely immersed in his own thoughts, continues: "If only I had known what I should come to. But I believed so much in myself, believed in my own strength. I wanted to go my own way. I was afraid of nothing. I threw away everything that people value and I never looked back. But now I would give half my life to go back and become like other people."

He rises and paces up and down the room.

The old man sits watching him, nodding his head and smiling. There is amusement and irony in his look—not an unsympathetic irony, but one full of understanding, of compassion and pity, as though he would like to help but cannot.

"I have always laughed at everything," continues Osokin, "and I have even enjoyed breaking up my life. I felt myself stronger than other people. Nothing could bend me, nothing could make me own myself beaten. I'm not beaten. But I can't fight any more. I've got myself into a sort of bog. I can't make a single movement. You understand me? I have to keep still and watch myself being sucked down."

The old man sits and looks at him.

"How has it come to this?" he says.

"How? You know so much about me that you must know this quite well. I was cast adrift when I was expelled from school. That alone changed my whole life. Because of that I am out of touch with everything. Take my schoolfellows: some are still at the University; others have taken their degrees, but each one of them has firm ground under his feet.

I have lived ten times more than they have, I know more, have read and seen a hundred times more than they have—and yet I am a man whom people treat with condescension."

"And is that all?" asks the old man.

"Yes, all—though not quite all. I had other chances, but one after another they slipped by me. The first was the most important. How terrible it is that quite without understanding or intention, when we are still too young to realize what the result may be, we can do things that affect our whole life and change our whole future. What I did at school was just a practical joke: I was bored. If I had known and understood what it would lead to, do you think I should have done it?"

The old man nods his head in assent. "Yes, you would have done it," he says.

"Never!"

The old man laughs.

Osokin continues to pace up and down the room, then stops and speaks again.

"And, later on, why did I quarrel with my uncle? The old man was really quite well-disposed towards me, but it was as though I provoked him on purpose by disappearing for whole days in the woods with the girl, his ward. True, Tanechka was extraordinarily sweet and I was only sixteen and our kisses were so beautiful. But the old man was mortally offended when he caught us kissing in the dining-room. How foolish it all was! If I had known what would come of it, do you not think I should have stopped?"

The magician laughs again. "You did know," he says.

Osokin stands smiling as though he were seeing and remembering something far away.

"It may be that I did know," he says. "Only it seemed so exciting then. But of course I ought not to have done it. And if I had known clearly what would happen, I should certainly have kept away from Tanechka."

"You did know quite clearly," says the old man. "Think and you will see."

"Of course I did not," says Osokin. "The whole trouble is that we never know for certain what is coming. If we knew definitely what would be the result of our actions, do you suppose we should do all that we do?"

"You always know," says the old man, looking at Osokin. "A man may not know what will happen as a result of other people's actions or as the result of unknown causes, but he always knows all possible results of his own actions."

Osokin becomes lost in thought and a shadow crosses his face.

"It may be," he says, "that sometimes I did foresee events. But one cannot take this as a rule . . . And besides I always approached life rather differently from other people."

The magician smiles. "I have never met a man yet," he says, "who was not convinced that he approached life rather differently from other people."

"But even I," continues Osokin without listening, "if I knew for certain what would come of it, why should I have done all these things? Take what happened at Military School. I realize that it was difficult for me there because I was not accustomed to discipline, but after all, that was absurd. I could have made myself bear it. Everything had begun to go smoothly and only a short time remained. Then suddenly, as though on purpose, I began to be late returning from leave. One Sunday, another—and then they told me that I should be expelled if I were late once more. Twice after that I came back in time, and then that evening at Leontieff's— the girl in the black dress—and I did not turn up at School at all. Well, what is the use of going over all that? As a result I was expelled. But I did not know beforehand that it would end like that!"

"You did know," the magician repeats.

Osokin laughs. "Well suppose that in this case I did know, but I was terribly bored with all that nonsense, and after all one always hopes for the best. I want you to understand that when I speak about *knowing*, I do not mean the sort of knowing which, in reality, is only supposition. I mean that if we knew with absolute certainty what was going to happen, then we should act differently."

"My dear friend, you do not realize what you are saying. If you knew something with absolute certainty, that would mean that it was inevitable. Then none of your actions could alter anything in any way. Sometimes you know things like this: you know, for instance, that if you touch fire you will burn yourself. But I do not mean that. I mean that you always know what results will come from one or another of your actions; but in a strange way you want to do one thing and get the result that could only come from another."

"We don't always know all the results we shall get," says Osokin.

"Always."

"Wait a moment, did I really know everything when I was a private soldier in Turkestan? I had no hopes whatever. Yet I was waiting for something."

The magician smiles again. "There was nothing you could do," he says. "Nothing depended on you, and you did nothing."

"Suddenly I received a legacy from an aunt," continues Osokin. "Thirty thousand roubles. That was my salvation. At first, I began by acting sensibly. I went abroad; I travelled for some time. Then I started going to lectures at the Sorbonne. Everything became possible again—many things were even better than before, and then in a silly moment, senselessly and stupidly, I lost all that remained of my money at roulette in the company of rich English and American students who did not even notice it. Did I know what I was doing then? Yet I was losing everything at that moment. I am sure that if we knew where we were going, we should very often stop."

The old man gets up and leaning on his stick, stands in front of Osokin.

"But you lost considerable sums of money before, at cards

and roulette," he says. "You told me so yourself. Why did only a third of your legacy remain?"

"Oh, I didn't lose all the money at cards. I had lived for four years abroad," answered Osokin. "And in any case, I couldn't live on my income. I still had enough to get my degree and then find some work."

"Yes," says the magician, "that may be, but you were losing your money already, and it was inevitable that you should lose it all. And you knew that you would lose it. You always know, but you never stop."

Osokin shakes his head impatiently.

"Of course not! Of course not!" he cries. "If only we could know! Our misfortune is that we crawl about like blind kittens on top of a table, never knowing where the edge is. We do absurd things because we know nothing that lies ahead of us. If we only could know! If only we could see a little ahead!"

He walks up and down the room, then stops in front of the old man.

"Listen, can't your magic do this for me? Can't you send me back? I have been thinking about it for a long time and to-day, when I heard about Zinaida, I felt that this was the only thing left for me. I cannot go on living. I have spoiled everything. Send me back if it is possible. I shall do everything differently. I shall live in a new way and I shall be prepared for meeting Zinaida when the time comes. I want to go back about ten years, to the time when I was still a schoolboy. Tell me, is it possible?"

The old man nods.

"It is possible," he says.

Osokin stops in amazement. "Can you do it?"

The old man nods again, and says: "I can do it, but it will not make things any better for you."

"Well, that is my affair," says Osokin. "Only send me back ten, no, twelve years, but there must be a condition that I shall remember everything—everything, you understand, including the smallest details. All that I have acquired during these twelve years must remain with me, all that I know, all my experience, all my knowledge of life. One could do anything then!"

"I can send you back as far as you like, and you will remember everything, but nothing will come of it," says the old man.

"How could nothing come of it?" says Osokin excitedly. "The whole horror of the thing is that we do not know our way. If I know and remember, I shall do everything differently. I shall have an aim, I shall be aware of the use and the necessity for all the difficult things I have to do. What are you saying? Of course I shall change my whole life. I shall find Zinaida while I am still at school. She will know nothing, but I shall know already that we have to meet later, and I shall do everything with this in view. Do you think I will again play all those tricks with my life? Certainly not!"

The old man sits down slowly and continues to look at him.

"Do it, if it is possible," says the old man. "You will go back twelve years as you wish. And you will remember everything *as long as you do not wish to forget.* Are you ready?"

"Quite ready," says Osokin. "In any case, I cannot go back home again. That, I feel, is impossible."

The old man claps his hands three times. A Chinese, the magician's servant, comes noiselessly into the room. He has a long pigtail, and is dressed in a blue silk gown trimmed with fur and shoes with thick felt soles. The magician speaks to him in a low voice. The Chinese, moving silently, brings in and places before the magician a small brazier of burning charcoal and a tall vase. The cat jumps down from the back of the magician's chair and walks out behind the Chinese. The old man dips one hand into the vase and with the other hand waves Osokin to the armchair. Osokin sits down.

Looking into the fire, the old man slowly pronounces some incomprehensible words, then, taking his hand out of the vase, he throws a handful of grey-green powder into the brazier. At the same time he takes the hour-glass from the table, shakes it and turns it over. Aromatic and pungent smoke rises in a cloud above the brazier.

The whole room fills with smoke, and in it can be seen many moving forms as though the room were suddenly full of people.

When the smoke clears away, the old man is sitting in his armchair holding the hour-glass in his hand.

There is no Osokin.

CHAPTER VI
MORNING

AN EARLY MORNING in October 1890.

A dormitory in a boys' school. Rows of beds. Sleeping figures rolled up in blankets. Through an archway another part of the dormitory can be seen. Lamps are burning. Outside it is still dark. A clock strikes six. A school servant nicknamed "Frog," a veteran of the Caucasian wars, appears at the far end of the dormitory and begins to ring a large bell as he walks along the wide center passage between the beds.

The dormitory comes to life at once. There is movement and noise. Some of the boys jump up, throw off their blankets and others try to snatch another half minute's sleep. A boy about thirteen jumps on his bed and begins to dance. Someone throws a pillow at him from the other end of the dormitory. The housemaster, a lanky German with a red beard, in a blue tailcoat with brass buttons, walks from one bed to another giving a tug at the blankets of those who are not getting up.

In a bed by the wall Ivan Osokin is sitting up staring about him in amazement. He looks like a boy of fourteen.

"Did I dream all that and what did it mean?" he says to himself. "And what I see now, is this too a dream?

"I went to the magician and asked him to send me back. He said he would send me back twelve years. Is it possible that this is true? I took a revolver and went out of the house. I couldn't stay at home. Is it really true that Zinaida is going to marry Minsky? What a queer dream! The dormitory looks absolutely like a real one. I am not sure whether I want to find myself here in reality or not; it was pretty beastly here

too. But how can I go on living? There is no Zinaida for me
any more. I can't accept that, I never shall. I told the magician I wanted to change my whole life and that I must begin
again, a long way back. But supposing he really did send me
back? It is impossible! I know it's a dream. But I will try to
imagine that I actually am at school . . . Is it better now or
worse? I don't even know what to say. Why does it make me
feel so frightened and so sad? After all, it can't be so . . . But
Zinaida . . . no, it really is a vicious circle, and I am indeed a
schoolboy, which means I dreamed it all—Zinaida and everything else. Can that be true or not? Well, there are a thousand
things I did not know and could not have known when I was
at school. I'll test this at once. What shall I try to remember?
I know! That time I did not know English. I learned it later.
If I know it now, it means that everything has been real, that
I have been abroad and all the rest of it. How does that tale
of Stevenson's begin about a King's daughter who had no
power over the morrow? 'The Song of the Morrow'? Yes,
that's right.

"*The King of Duntrine had a daughter when he was old, and
she was the fairest King's daughter between two seas . . .*

"So it's all true. I do know English. I can remember how it
goes on:

". . . *her hair was like spun gold, and her eyes like pools in a
river; and the King gave her a castle upon the sea beach, with
a terrace, and a court of hewn stone, and four towers at the
four corners.*

"But then, that means that all this is a dream . . ."

"Osokin, Osokin," shouts his friend Memorsky. "Why are
you sitting there like an owl? Have you fallen asleep? Don't
you hear, the German is taking the names of those who are
not dressed. Wake up, you devil's puppet!" Osokin seizes the
pillow and throws it angrily at the laughing Memorsky, who
neatly dodges it.

At that moment the German housemaster comes out from
behind the archway and the pillow, flying over Memorsky's

head, hits him full in the face. He staggers with the unexpect-edness of the blow, then rushes furiously at Osokin.

The German has a habit of grabbing them with his own hands and dragging them to some place where they have to stand for punishment: 'under the clock' or 'under the lamp' or 'by the bookcase' or simply 'by the wall.' The boys do not regard the punishment as a disgrace, but 'being grabbed' by the German is considered both ridiculous and humiliating.

At first, Osokin looks helplessly at the German and wants to explain what happened, but, seeing his furious face and realizing his intention, turns pale and puts out his hands to defend himself. The German, noticing this movement just in time and the expression on Osokin's face, stops. For a few moments they stand facing each other. A circle of interested onlookers rapidly forms around them. The German is chok-ing with rage, but he controls himself and decides to make things as disagreeable as possible for Osokin.

"Why are you not dressed?" he shouts at him. "How much longer will such scandalous behavior go on? Fighting from the first thing in the morning! You are keeping everyone waiting. I'll tell the servants to wash you if you don't want to wash yourself. Make haste and dress, and go under the clock. You will have no breakfast and during preparation you will stand by the bookcase. Afterwards I will speak to Gustav Lukitch. Now, dress!"

The German turns sharply and goes out. The boys disperse, some of them laughing, others sympathizing with Osokin and shouting encouragement to him. Osokin nervously begins to dress.

"How perfectly absurd," the thought flits across his mind. "What an idiotic dream! Fancy seeing that ugly face again. But why am I dressing? I'll lie down and stay in bed. Of course this is a dream."

But at that moment he remembers the magician and he feels so amazed that he can hardly keep himself from laughing aloud.

"I can imagine what the magician would say! This is indeed a brilliant way to begin a new life. And it is curious, this is exactly what happened before. I remember that affair of the pillow perfectly. But how could I know that this was going to happen to-day? The magician would be sure to say: You knew. As a matter of fact something of the sort did flash through my mind just as I was going to throw the pillow. I could have stopped, I wanted to stop, and yet I threw it. Damn the German! Of course he had to turn up. Now he will complain to Gustav and altogether it's going to be a nasty business. This means that my leave will be stopped and possibly my conduct mark lowered as well. But why do I think about it? It cannot matter to me one way or the other. I am going to wake up at once. I must make an effort; there is nothing real in all this. I will wake up. Well—"

The German appears from behind the archway.

"Are you not ready yet?" he shouts at Osokin. "Prokofy, take him under the clock."

Another school servant, Prokofy, Osokin's great friend, also an old soldier, whom the boys call "Potato," walks reluctantly from the other end of the dormitory towards him. Realizing that of two evils one should choose the lesser, Osokin seizes a towel and, without looking at the German, walks rapidly out of the dormitory.

The landing between the junior and senior dormitories. A broad iron staircase leading to the lower floor. A round yellow clock on the wall. Under the clock stands Osokin, looking agitated and bewildered. Boys pass by him as they go to and fro. No one takes any notice of him.

"Am I going mad or am I mad already?" thinks Osokin. "There are no such dreams. Yet I cannot wake up. It is impossible that I'm really back at school. All this is too stupid. I know that if only I begin to think about my life, about Zinaida . . . I shall wake up; but I can't stop thinking about that idiotic German and being kept in on Saturday. That is why I go on sleeping. It would really be funny to come back to school in order to be kept without leave as usual. No, this is absurd. If I actually did return, at any rate I should get the most that could be got out of it; and I must say that it would be interesting to see Zinaida as a little girl. I even know at which school she was. But can it really be true that she is going to marry Minsky and that she will be a complete stranger to me? Then why should I want to see her? There is one thing I don't understand; why is this stupid dream dragging on so long? Usually, in a dream, the moment I begin to realize that I am dreaming, I wake up at once. Now, for some reason, I can't wake up. I know what I'll do. I'll jump downstairs over the banisters. If I float in the air it will mean that this is a dream. After all, it can't be reality, so I can't fall."

Osokin with a long stride, walks resolutely across the landing, takes hold of the iron banister and looks down. At that moment, several boys of about his own age run out of the dormitory. When they see Osokin leaning over the banisters they rush at him and fall on him from behind. They all laugh.

Osokin tries to free himself and accidentally hits one of his assailants in the face with his elbow. The boy is evidently in great pain. He yells and puts his hands to his face. Blood trickles between his fingers. The other boys let go of Osokin and wait, curious to see what will happen next. The German comes out of the senior boys' dormitory and takes in the situation at a glance. Osokin, who was being punished, in this case by being put under the clock, and who had no right to move without permission, has left his place, taken part in a fight and broken Klementieff's nose.

Osokin, realizing that all the evidence is against him, tries to say something, but the German will not let him speak.

"Again a fight, and again Osokin," he shouts. "To begin with, who allowed you to move from your place? No, this is beyond everything!" The German works himself up more and more.

"Must we chain you or put you in a cage? Or put a straitjacket on you? You cannot be left alone for a moment. Enough! I have no nurses for you. When the others go to the dining-room you will stay here under the clock and you will stand there during preparation until Gustav Lukitch comes. He can do what he likes with you. I give it up. And if you move from here again, I shall send you to the infirmary."

Osokin is annoyed and disgusted with everything that is happening, at the same time he is extremely amused at the sight of the German. He wants to say something which will make him understand that he, Osokin, is not a schoolboy and that this is only a dream, but nothing occurs to him. But in spite of himself he feels disturbed by the German's threats, as if something thoroughly unpleasant were lying in wait for him.

Osokin is standing under the clock again.

At the other end of the landing, boys begin to form up in pairs: junior boys in front, seniors behind. There are about a hundred of them altogether.

"Prokofy," shouts the German, "Osokin is to stand there under the clock. If he moves from his place, come and tell me."

The German throws a spiteful glance at Osokin, then slowly walks down the stairs ahead of the boys. The boys follow after him in pairs, taking no notice of Osokin.

"Osokin, I'll 'bring out' for you," shouts Memorsky.

In schoolboy language this means that Memorsky will bring a roll—or a piece of one—to Osokin, who is going to be left without breakfast.

CHAPTER VII
THOUGHTS

OSOKIN IS LEFT ALONE. In spite of himself, the alarmed feeling of a schoolboy who has done something wrong and expects punishment gains possession of him more and more, and he cannot get rid of it.

To be left alone in the dormitory and "under the clock" during breakfast and for the whole of preparation is not an ordinary punishment that can be disregarded. And to be sent to the infirmary is the most that a housemaster can threaten on his own authority. The infirmary in itself is not in the least frightening. On the contrary, it is a very pleasant place; but to be sent there when one is well means separation from the others, and it is the usual preliminary to being expelled from school.

The school servants, all old soldiers, are cleaning up the dormitories. From the landing both the senior and the junior dormitories can be seen.

"First of all, I don't believe any of this," says Osokin to himself, and "secondly, I want to smoke," he concludes unexpectedly.

"I wonder if I have any cigarettes." He fumbles in his pockets. "Not one. A watch, a silver twenty-kopeck piece, a penknife, a candle, and a burning glass, a comb, a pencil and that's all."

Osokin cannot help smiling at these contents of a schoolboy's pockets.

"The devil only knows what things one can dream about!" he says. "But it's astonishing how the whole thing is coming back to me step by step. This is exactly how everything happened before: I hit the German with the pillow, I smashed Klementieff's nose, and I believe I even looked for a cigarette as I stood under the clock. But yesterday I could not have recalled all this and told it with such detail. And now I even remember what happened afterwards. Gustav came and lectured me, my conduct mark was lowered and then I was kept without leave for three Sundays. This drove me wild and I gave up working altogether. So this was the beginning of a whole series of pleasant events which ended in my being stuck in the fourth form for a second year. If I've come back to set all this right I could hardly have chosen a better beginning. But this is all nonsense. What do I care about the school? I shall wake up and that will be the end of it. It's simply a memory that has floated up in some unaccountable way—I had better think about the present."

He tries to think about Zinaida but he feels such a pang in his heart that he shakes his head and says to himself:

"No, anything but that; that's what I ran away from. I don't care whether this is a dream or not, but I cannot bear to think of Zinaida. So what can I think of? Everything is damned bad—both here and there. But this is impossible. I must find something to fix my mind on, otherwise it's quite unbearable . . . Who was it who came to see me yesterday? Why, Stoupitsyn of course. I can imagine how he would laugh if I told him the magician had sent me back to school. I don't believe one could have a worse punishment. By the way, Stoupitsyn must be here too, only he's a day-boy. It would be interesting to see him. Anyhow, I must try to do something: dream or no dream, I don't want to stand under the clock. If I came back to school, it was certainly not for this. But it's an awfully strange dream; a kind of nightmare or delirium. Perhaps I am ill, perhaps I have typhus. It's strange that I can reason so coherently, but they say it happens like that sometimes. If so, I must find the beginning. When could this delirium have begun? I remember Stoupitsyn saying yesterday that I wasn't looking well. Then I went to the post and met Krutitsky. He told me about Zinaida. That was the beginning of it . . . But perhaps it didn't happen after all, perhaps I never went to the post and never met him; perhaps it's all delirium about Zinaida getting married. I was probably taken ill immediately after Stoupitsyn left, and am now lying delirious in my room—or in the hospital—and can't wake up. That's most likely what it is. Well, there's one thing, as soon as I recover, I'll go to the Crimea—without a ticket if need be, on the couplings or somehow, but go I shall . . . Perhaps it's not typhus but simply a fever like those I used to have before in Turkestan."

Prokofy, who is on very good terms with the boys, nods to him with a grin, as he comes by.

"Now you've got it, Osokin! What were you fighting about?"

Osokin does not understand him at first and then he involuntarily answers him in schoolboy's language:

"But we were not fighting. I only hit him with my elbow by accident."

Prokofy shakes his head. "Well, you got him all right. How his nose bled! It could hardly be stopped. They kept telling him to 'hold your nose up!' And now his nose is all blue and swollen up, like this!" Prokofy shows how big Klementieff's nose has become.

"But it was an accident," says Osokin, shuffling from one foot to the other.

"Oh, yes, and you flung a pillow at Wilhelm Petrovitch's head by accident too? Just you wait, Gustav Lukitch will prescribe for you!"

Prokofy waves his hand and goes into the dormitory.

The thread of Osokin's thought is broken.

"I cannot understand," he says. "What am I now—a schoolboy or a grown-up man? Yes, this is a repetition of everything that happened before, down to the smallest details. But then, if I have come back, it certainly was not for this. And if it's a dream, why does it last so long? How often have I dreamed of school before! And it was always awfully funny. I remember when I was in Paris I dreamed that I was back at school again. Everything was exactly as it is now. And I remember that I wanted to go out somewhere, and I asked Gustav and he wouldn't let me go. I said to him: 'I must go to see some people, Gustav Lukitch, it is connected with important business.' And he answered, with his funny Czech accent: 'That is no concern of mine. If you have entered the school, you must submit to all the rules.' Well, now it means that I shall have to have explanations with Gustav once more.

"But, damn it, I have to admit that it's all very amazing; only I must try not to forget this dream. One always forgets the most interesting part. Here is a subject for a poem: where does the dream end and where does reality begin? It is impossible to define. What we see appears to be reality, but afterwards we call that very same thing a dream.

"But I wonder whether this dream will go on long enough. If I knew for certain that it would last, I could turn it any way I like. How much one could see! Now let me think, whom would I like to see? Mother?"

Osokin stops in the middle of his thoughts and feels frightened.

"But she's dead," he says to himself, "I remember her funeral. How shall I look at her now? I'll be remembering all the time that I have seen her dead. I remember, even then at school, I used to think that the time would come when she would die and I asked myself what should I do. Then she really did die . . . and I did nothing and continued to live. The most awful thing is that we become resigned to everything. But how I should like to see her now! Why is this such a stupid dream? Why do I dream of the German, of Prokofy, and not of her? What a strange sensation! This is exactly what happened constantly at school before. I remember the thought used to come to me sometimes then, that mother might die, and I wanted desperately to see her at once, at that very moment to be at home, to sit beside her and talk to her. And now it's the same thing again. I don't know what I wouldn't give just to see her now. But I suppose I shall be kept in on Saturday. What nonsense all this is! Why do I think about it? I can't be prevented from doing what I want by these dreams. I want to see her, I must! Once again it's all the same as it was before. How bored I used to be when I was kept in at weekends! These thick-skinned creatures cannot understand what it means to sit here for a week and not be able to go home on Saturday. It's the only thing that makes life here possible. But what can I do to see Mother? It is necessary but at the same time it frightens me. How shall I look at her and speak to her now, remembering her funeral? Now I understand why I always used to have such a feeling of pity for her. It was a presentiment."

Osokin stands for a long time immersed in his thoughts.

"I cannot get it into my head," he says looking round. "I want to understand: is this a dream or not?"

CHAPTER VIII
THE PAST

ON THE SCREEN are seen a series of pictures of school life.

The morning continues. Before lessons Osokin is called to the assistant headmaster, Gustav Lukitch, a fat Czech, who gives him a long lecture. Osokin tries to explain to him what has happened but he refuses to listen and threatens Osokin with all sorts of terrible punishments. In the end, for all the offences committed in the morning, Osokin has his leave stopped for three Sundays.

Lessons begin. Osokin does not even know what preparation has been set. Lowest marks for Greek. The other lessons pass by safely; he is not questioned.

Osokin sits through each lesson and moves during the breaks as though he were in a daze. It is painful to think of himself as a grown man, for then all his thoughts are occupied with Zinaida; but equally painful to think of himself as a schoolboy, for then he thinks of his mother and that she must soon die.

After lessons the boarders change into holland blouses and go downstairs. They are not going out, because the weather is bad. It happens sometimes, in autumn, that the boarders do not go out for three weeks at a time. What pleasure is there for the master in splashing about in the mud or walking in the rain? And as there are five masters, and a different one is on duty every day, each of them thinks that one of the others will be taking the boys out. And, after all, what does it matter if the boys stay indoors for a day or two? It never occurs to anyone that week after week passes in this way. And the assistant headmaster and the headmaster do not want to know anything about it. They do not come to the school until the evening.

The boys scatter all over the big school building. The younger ones run downstairs to the gymnasium.

Osokin sits on a window sill on the first floor and gazes into the street. Everything is just the same. There is the sign 'Sausages and Cheese,' and next to it, 'Meat and Fish.' Mud, rain, a disgusting late Moscow autumn. Horse-trams, the jaded horses streaming with rain, and carriages with their hoods up, pass by. Osokin feels miserable and sad. He would like to find himself at home sitting with his mother, reading or listening to her reading aloud. Or it would be nice to go somewhere, to wander about the streets in the rain; sometimes this too is very pleasant. Perhaps he might even see Zinaida! Again those same thoughts!

"But then, after all, is this a dream or is it reality?" he asks himself. "What can prove that it is a dream? English? Yes, because I could not have known it before. I began to learn it in Petersburg. How does that tale begin?

"The King of Duntrine had a daughter when he was old, and she was the fairest King's daughter between two seas . . ."

He recalls the words of Stevenson's fable further in broken snatches.

"I can't remember it all," says Osokin to himself. "I must get hold of Stevenson. But it's very curious—if I'm a schoolboy, how do I know this? And I know that I was in London and lived in a boarding house near the British Museum; and in Paris I know every corner and turning in Montmartre and on the Rive Gauche. No, I will try to pretend that I am not asleep, that the magician has actually sent me back as I wished so that I can arrange my life in a new way. What then must I do? Everything has got to be different. I must finish school; and to do that I must work and avoid such adventures as happened this morning. Of course, it will be difficult for me at first, but in a day or two I shall get used to it. I am in the fourth form now. That means I shall finish school when I am eighteen and go to the University. By the time I meet Zinaida I shall have taken my degree. That will make all the difference. But what a very long time it will take. And how boring it is here—simply deadly. Yes, I understand perfectly why I could not work and why I never finished school. How am I to endure this boredom? I must think of how I shall go to the Crimea with Zinaida. How wonderful that will be! In the evening we will sit side by side in the train and watch the fields go by—then the steppes will begin, then the chalk hills, then the steppes again. Perhaps I shall get to know her sooner . . . Of course I really ought to see her now. She is here in Moscow. She won't know it, but I shall see her from time to time. But how could she agree to marry Minsky? It was my fault. She really must have thought that I didn't come because I was interested in someone else; but now all that will be different."

His friend Sokoloff comes up to him. Sokoloff is a little younger than Osokin and one form lower, but for some reason he is the only one to whom Osokin can talk.

"What are you dreaming about, Osokin?"

"Do you know, Sokoloff," says Osokin, "you're going to be a lawyer."

"What nonsense! I'm going to the Engineering Institute."

"Nothing of the sort, you're going to study law. And now guess what I'm going to be?"

"If you're going to spend your time like to-day, beating Wilhelm in the face with a pillow and getting at least one bad mark a day, you're most likely going to be a tramp or a rogue of some sort. Well, maybe for old acquaintance' sake I'll find you a signalman's job."

"Well, we'll see," says Osokin.

"There's nothing to see in it. It's as clear as daylight that you'll never finish school."

"Why do you speak so confidently?"

"Because you do nothing."

"It's awfully dull here," says Osokin. "But still I have

made up my mind to work. For nothing on earth will I stay another year in the same form."

Sokoloff laughs. "How many times have I heard that! For two months now you've been getting ready to begin to work. Well, tell me, what is set for Greek to-morrow?"

"You grind!" says Osokin, laughing. "And do you know, you are going to have a red beard."

"Well, tell me some more lies. Why should I have a red beard—my hair is black."

"Yes, you will have a red beard and you will be a lawyer. I dreamed it."

"Let's go down," says Sokoloff.

They go off together.

A few days later. Evening preparation in school. Rows of desks. Through the open door the junior boys' room can be seen. Lamps are burning. The boys are preparing lessons. Osokin, determined to begin to work, has drawn up a program for himself and is repeating Latin grammar. After reading a page, he shuts the book and looking straight in front of him repeats in his mind: "*Cupio, desidero, opto, volo, appeto* . . . Damn! What does *appeto* mean?"

He looks in the grammar.

"Oh yes . . . Well, and then: *Volo, nolo, appeto, expecto, posso, postulo, impetro, adipiscor, experior, praestolor* . . . *Praestolor* . . . ! Again I've forgotten!"

He looks at the book, then yawns and looks around.

"It's devilish boring. Yes, now I understand why I could never work before. Fancy inventing such absurdity as to make us learn bald grammar! And yet this same Latin could be very interesting. I remember those lectures at the Sorbonne. I went there to study psychology and became quite infatuated with Latin poetry . . . And now this school Latin is ten times more boring for me than it was before. Well, I must say that I have got myself into a mess. And I must make the most of it. But how sickening that I have to sit here for three weeks! How interesting it would be to see Moscow. Strange that I didn't realize how dull and boring it would be here. It seems that I can do nothing about it after all. And it was just as dull and just as boring then . . ."

In the junior classroom, where the master sits, a noise begins; everyone gets up. First preparation is over. Two of Osokin's friends, Telehoff and a Pole called Brahovsky, come up to him.

"Have you done your lessons?" asks Brahovsky, laughing.

"Yes."

"You're lying. I've been watching you for the last half hour. I can't even make out what you were doing. I could understand it if you were reading something, but you just stare at the book; you're not learning a thing, that's obvious. You just sit and stare at one spot."

"Listen, Brahovsky," says Osokin, "do you know the story about the Pole and the Khokhol*? The Pole said to the Khokhol: 'You're a lazy man. For three hours I've sat watching you and you've done nothing at all!' And the Khokhol said: 'And what were you doing during that time, *panie*'?"

They all laugh, except Osokin, who looks at Brahovsky in perplexity as a fresh whirl of thoughts surges through his mind. He does not hear the rest of what Brahovsky is saying.

"I remember quite clearly," he says to himself. "We stood here before, exactly like this, and Brahovsky said the same thing—that he couldn't understand how I could sit and stare at a book, and I told him the same story. This shows how easy it is to slip into the old groove. No, all this must be changed."

At these words he comes to a stop.

"It seems to me," he says, "that even then I always repeated to myself that everything must be changed."

A few days later. Evening preparation again. Osokin feels very bored and very divided in himself.

* A little Russian, a Ukrainian.

"I must get out of this," he says to himself. "After all, there are many moments in a day when one can simply walk out of the school. Why did I not do so at once? All this idea of returning is absurd. I just cannot stay here any more. I don't understand this situation and I don't believe in it, but, even if I was stupid enough to return here, the sooner I get away the better; if there is a possibility of change, this change can only begin by my getting away from school at any price. I must simply run away from here."

But somehow, even while saying all this, Osokin knows that he will never do it.

"It would be too simple if we could do such things," he says to himself again. "There is something in us that keeps us where we find ourselves. I think this is the most awful thing of all."

But he doesn't want to think. For some time he sits without thoughts, then imperceptibly he slips into the fantastic dreams which, in the past, were responsible for many unprepared lessons and for many bad marks. The dreams are called 'Travels in Oceanis.' They are his best method of running away from reality.

Osokin is sailing in the Pacific. The ship, in a storm, strikes a rock and is wrecked. Osokin, half dead, is thrown by a wave on the shore of an unknown country. He is found, brought to a house, revived and fed by the inhabitants.

When Osokin recovers fully he becomes keenly interested in these people. Very soon he realizes that they are not like any others in the world. They are a very cultured and civilized race. They have founded an ideal state where there is no poverty, no crime, no stupidity and no cruelty. Everyone is happy there; they all enjoy life: the sunshine, nature, art. 'Travels in Oceanis' is made up from half a dozen books he has read, but for Osokin there is something very personal and exciting about Oceanis. Many interesting things happen to him there.

One or two of the inhabitants of Oceanis—sometimes it is a

girl with a cheerful, happy face—act as his guides, showing him various institutions of the country and explaining its social organization. They go down into the crater of an extinct volcano; they climb snowy mountain peaks; they have dozens of strange and unexpected adventures. Sometimes, when his guide is the girl with the cheerful face, Osokin finds himself in very complicated situations; either they have to spend the night in the same room in the solitary rest-house; or rain and thunder in the mountains drive them to take shelter in a cave; or the boat in which they are crossing a river capsizes and they climb on to a small island and have to dry their clothes before a fire. On several of these occasions, Osokin's companion undresses and dresses in front of him without the slightest embarrassment—and this naturalness and freedom from restraint pleases him particularly and excites his imagination.

While some adventure of this kind is taking place in Oceanis, Osokin is incapable of being interested in anything else on earth.

"Why am I thinking about all this nonsense again?" he asks himself irresolutely. "Because there is nothing else to think about," he replies. "After all, everything is equally absurd."

But after some time, with a curious feeling of interest, he notices a definite difference in his dreams. He seems to be divided. One part of him continues to drift, inventing even more extravagant adventures and new subjects for talk with the inhabitants of Oceanis while another part observes the formation of dreams and draws its own conclusions. The dreams themselves also change perceptibly. First, the adventures with the young ladies of Oceanis become less innocent and acquire a much more experienced character, and second, Osokin finds that his attitude towards Oceanis itself and its people has changed completely.

In the old days—or as he says to himself, *then*—his attitude was full of curiosity and admiration; now it is ironical, unbelieving and argumentative. He realizes that not only has he lost the capacity to believe in Utopias or enjoy them, but he has definitely acquired some kind of distrust of them, some suspicion that there is intentional lying—or at least a voluntary suppression of the truth. His talks with the 'party people' in Switzerland, in Paris and in Moscow, and the unpleasant feeling which they always left in him are now definitely reflected in all that happens in Oceanis.

He smiles involuntarily when he realizes that *now* he tries to prove to the inhabitants of Oceanis that they cannot be such as they pretend themselves to be.

"You are frauds," he says to them. "You cannot exist in reality. Even in imagination you can be thought of only in impossible conditions."

"We only show what is possible for all people and in any country," replies an inhabitant of Oceanis with whom he happens to be talking at the moment.

"You show exactly what is impossible for all people or any country," says Osokin. "To exist, you need bad logic and artificial conditions such as cannot be created in real life; and any attempt to bring into being a social organization like yours will only result in the destruction of everything that is more or less decent, and in general misery."

Suddenly Osokin stops and his expression changes.

"But here is proof that I've come back from a quite different life," he says to himself. "I never thought like that before. I was rather enticed by Utopias. Now I know it's all just a fake—and a very cheap fake. This is very interesting. I have been looking for proof. This is definite proof. I never could have thought like that before."

Preparation ends. Osokin walks in a noisy crowd of boys, full of his new thoughts and his sudden discovery; and he feels rather sad. Oceanis will no longer be as attractive as it was before. Probably it will disappear—like his other dreams in which he imagined himself a famous general or famous poet or a great painter.

Some days later. Night. The school dormitory. Osokin is lying on a hard bed under a red blanket. The faint light of a lamp half turned down comes from the far side of the dormitory.

"I understand nothing," Osokin says to himself. "Now everything seems to be a dream, both the present and the past. I should like to wake up from both. I wish I could be somewhere in the South where there is sea, sunshine and freedom. I should like to think of nothing, expect nothing, remember nothing. But how strange! The magician said I should remember everything until I wished to forget; and already I want to forget. It seems to me that during these last days I have forgotten a great deal. I can't bear it. It's too painful for me to think of Zinaida. Maybe this is a dream? No, it cannot be a dream; I really was there ... So everything that is happening now was the past then; and what happened then is now the past. What surprises me most is that I take it so calmly, without even being particularly astonished—as though everything were just as it ought to be. But what can I do? Perhaps we accept all extraordinary things in this way. However astonished we may be, nothing changes, and we begin to pretend that it does not seem astonishing to us at all. When my grandmother died, I thought: what an inexplicable and extraordinary thing death is! But everyone takes it for granted. What else can they do? I remember thinking, during the funeral, that if all the people on earth suddenly disappeared and only one man remained, then for one day it would seem terrible and astonishing to him—but the next day he would probably think that it was quite normal and inevitable.

"How strange to find myself at school again! I remember these sounds of breathing, each one different, just like clocks ticking in a watchmaker's shop. I remember that I often lay awake at night then, too, and listened. What does it all mean? I wish I could understand!"

CHAPTER IX
A DREAM

Osokin dreams that after lessons, while he and Sokoloff are walking in the gymnasium talking about something or other, he is unexpectedly called to the reception room. His mother sometimes comes in to see him about this time, so he goes up the stairs and through the long corridors without expecting anything unusual.

In the reception room he sees a beautifully dressed young lady who is quite unknown to him. He stops in confusion, acutely aware of his ink-stained holland blouse, the tufts of hair sticking out from the back of his head, and his whole schoolboy appearance.

He has evidently been sent for in mistake for someone else; but the young lady looks at him, laughs, and holds out a small hand in a yellow suède glove.

"Heavens, how big you have grown!" she says. "And you don't seem to recognize me."

Osokin looks at her and does not know what to say. She is very attractive with large sparkling eyes. He feels still more awkward. He would like to say something pleasant, but he is ready to wager that this is the first time in his life that he has seen her. For some reason it seems to him that she is making fun of him by saying that he has grown so big—as though she had known him before. But for what purpose, he does not understand.

"Well, don't you know me?" she says in a clear, girlish and singularly pleasant voice. "Think, and you will remember." She looks at him and laughs.

For a single instant, quicker than the quickest thought, a

recollection flashes through Osokin's mind. Yes, he does know her. Why had he not realized it at once? But when could he have known her?

Osokin quickly searches through the memory of his whole life up to the moment when he went to the magician and he can say with certainty that she was not in that life.

"Oh, how funny you are!" she says. "So you've completely forgotten me. Don't you remember me at Zvenigorod? I was older than you were; you remember, I had a red ribbon in my plait. Don't you remember how we drove to the mill and how, another time, we went to look for Joutchka?"

Osokin remembers Zvenigorod where he lived with his father and mother when he was quite a little child; he re-members the water mill in the forest and the smell of the flour, the smell of tar from the boats by the ferry, the white monastery on the hill and the wood with the ice-cold springs above the road; and Joutchka?—the little black dog who once disappeared and couldn't be found for a long time. But there was no girl with a red ribbon there. Of this he is quite firmly convinced. He feels again that she is making fun of him. But why? Who is she? How does she know about Zvenigorod and Joutchka?

He is silent and she continues to laugh her infectious laugh. She takes him by the hand and makes him sit down beside her. He becomes aware of the scent she uses—a faint but strangely penetrating perfume. This scent at once tells him an extraordinary number of things. Yes, of course he knows her. But where and when has he seen her? Maybe she was part of some other dream. He recognizes this sensation: when dreaming he remembers another dream.

"Why are you so silent?" she asks. "Say something. Are you glad to see me?"

"I am glad," says Osokin, flushing painfully and feeling quite unable to stop being a schoolboy. "Why are you glad?"

"Because I love you," says Osokin, not knowing where the courage comes from to say it and at the same time burning with the agonizing shame of being a schoolboy while she is a grown-up young lady.

She laughs outright now, and her eyes laugh and the dimple in her cheek laughs as well.

"Since when have you loved me?" she asks.

"I have always loved you," answers Osokin. "Even that time at Zvenigorod," and somehow this lie seems necessary.

She gives him a quick look, and immediately something is understood and accepted between them. It is as though they had agreed about it together.

"Very well," she says, "but what shall we do now? I came here because I couldn't find you anywhere else."

Osokin realizes that she has been looking for him *there*— but where *there* is he cannot say. He understands that, for some reason, this need not be said more plainly.

"Well, then," she says, "are you going to stay here?"

"No," answers Osokin, to his own surprise, "certainly not! We'll run away. I mean, I shall run away with you. We'll go downstairs together, and while you are putting on your things in the hall, I'll put on someone's coat and go out to the front steps. Then we'll take a carriage and drive away."

"Well, let's go," she says, just as though everything had been decided between them long ago.

There is something Osokin both understands and does not understand, and a whirl of new expectations fills his whole being. It is so extraordinarily pleasant to feel, all at once, so many new things and so many unexpected changes. Ahead, there again lies something new, something that has never happened before, something sparkling and filled with brilliant colors.

They come out to the landing and go down the stairs. The staircase is long and dark, and quite unlike the one that leads to the hall.

"We've come to the wrong staircase," says Osokin.

"It doesn't matter" she whispers softly. "This one will lead us straight out." In the darkness she puts her arms round his neck and, laughing softly, presses his head to her.

Osokin is aware of the touch of her arms, he feels the silk and fur against his face; he is aware of her scent and the soft, warm tender contact of the woman. His arms go round her hesitatingly. He feels the soft firm breasts beneath her dress and corset. A painfully sweet tremor seizes his whole body. His lips are pressed to her cheek and he hears how quickly she is breathing. Her lips find his. "Is this really true?" asks a voice inside Osokin. "Yes, of course," another voice replies. A wild joy fills him. It seems to him that in that moment they separate themselves from the earth and fly.

Suddenly at the top of the stairs a harsh and disagreeable bell begins to ring and voices are heard. A painful feeling at once grips Osokin's heart. She is now going to disappear.

"We are too late," she says quickly, freeing herself from Osokin's arms.

Osokin too feels that he has lost her, that something infinitely beautiful, radiant and joyful is escaping from him.

"Darling, listen! I must run or it will be too late. But I shall come again. Wait for me, do you hear, don't forget . . ."

She says something else as she runs swiftly down the stairs, but Osokin cannot hear her, for the bell, ringing louder and louder, drowns her voice. Already she is out of sight. Osokin wants to rush after her; he makes an effort to see where she has gone—and opens his eyes.

"The Frog," with his turned-out feet, is passing quite close to his bed, ringing a bell with an air of concentration.

It is morning.

Several seconds pass before Osokin comes to himself. He is filled with the happy tremor of the kiss, with the sharp anguish of its passing, and with the joy that it has happened.

What he has experienced is so utterly out of keeping with the dormitory, the shouts of the boys and the glaring light of the oil lamps. He is still acutely conscious of the scent, of the touch of arms around his neck, of soft hair brushing his cheek . . . All this is still with him. His heart is beating very fast. His whole body seems to have become alive and conscious of itself in a sort of happy wonder.

"Who is she?" is the first clear thought that comes, at last, to his mind. "She said she would come back. But when? Why did I not hear what she said to me at the end? What am I to do now?"

He is desperately sorry to lose his dream. It seems to him that he might still overtake her, and ask her who she is, where she comes from, and what is the meaning of all this mystery.

If *that* was real, then everything happening around him seems so unnecessary, so senseless and stupidly irritating. It is dreadful that another day is beginning and that he must live through it. At the same time, it is so good that it has happened—even if only in a dream. It means that it can happen again. Now, some golden rays are shining in the distance as though the sun were rising.

"But who is she, where does she come from?" he asks himself again. "I don't know her face—and yet I do know it. Or do I?"

All day Osokin goes about in a kind of mist, still under the influence of his dream. He wants to keep it all in his memory and to live this dream over and over again; he wants to understand who the unknown girl is. But the dream fades, grows pale, vanishes—yet something of it remains.

In the middle of the day, returning to his dream and comparing the memory of it with the impressions of life, Osokin suddenly realizes with amazement that the image of Zinaida has grown faint and shadowy. He can now recall her without any pain. Even yesterday it was different, for then a single thought of Zinaida caused him acute pain. As he realizes this, there flashes through his mind, for one ten-thousandth part of a second, not a recollection but a shadow of a recollection of a young girl with a red ribbon in her dark plait whom he was telling about Zvenigorod . . .

"So that is where she got it from," he says to himself. But in the same moment he feels that he has again forgotten everything. Only the realization remains that this happened at a time when everything connected with Zinaida already belonged to the past. Perhaps that too was a dream.

Once more his mind catches a certain thread of thought.

"Yes, yes," he says to himself, almost afraid to breathe. "Does it mean . . . could it have happened *afterwards*? But after what?"

And then, quite unexpectedly, his mind comes to a conclusion, and he says to himself—"This has not happened, *but it will happen if I go on living.*"

He does not fully understand this conclusion as yet, but his whole being is filled with gratitude to this girl for having come to him.

Having made this last effort, his mind refuses to understand any more. Osokin feels that his dream is quickly fading and disappearing, and that soon there will be almost nothing left of it. Until evening he keeps returning to the dream in his thoughts and several times he thinks that he has flashes of understanding of strange things.

"There is no essential difference between the past and the future," he thinks. "We only call them by different words: *was* and *will be*. In reality, all this both 'was' and 'will be'."

All day long the school and his surroundings seem utterly unreal, like transparent shadows. At times, it seems to Osokin that if he could lose himself deeply enough in thought, and then look around him, everything would become quite different—and perhaps the *continuation of his dream* would then begin.

CHAPTER X
THE SCHOOLBOY

SUNDAY. Winter. It is snowing. Osokin, a schoolboy in a grey overcoat with a black fur collar and silver buttons, and a dark blue cap with the silver school badge of laurel leaves, is walking down a small street near Pokrovsky Gate. He stops at a corner and looks about him.

"Yes, of course," he says, "here are all the old houses, just as they were before. But I have seen it quite changed. It is surprising how many changes can take place in twelve years. Well now, I must take a look round. The Krutitskys' new house doesn't exist yet but they are living somewhere near here. Oh, if I could see Zinaida! But how strange, what could I do even if I did see her? I am a schoolboy, she is a little girl. And the funny thing about it is that then, too, I used to wander about Moscow streets and alleys, and sometimes just here, feeling that I had to meet someone, find someone. But it is no use despairing beforehand. It would be good to see her, but I must certainly find her brother, and get to know him and make friends with him. He should be in a cadet corps, but which, I don't know. That has gone completely out of my head. I remember he told me a lot about his corps. Now I begin to forget everything! Yes, of course I must find him, otherwise we shall not meet each other at all. I hope this time I shall go to the University and not to the Military School. And besides, when we were in Military School, Zinaida had already gone abroad. This time we must certainly meet sooner.

"How strange it all is! Sometimes it seems as if my former

life, the magician and Zinaida, are all like 'Travels in Oceanis'. Well, we shall see."

He stops in front of a house and reads the name plate on the gate.

"This is the house. Now, what next?"

He looks into the courtyard.

"There is the front door; probably they live here."

A dvornik* crosses the courtyard. Osokin moves away and walks further along the street.

"I'll walk about here," he says to himself, "perhaps some-one will come out. It would be splendid if Krutitsky came out; I should speak to him at once. Confound it! I suddenly re-member that he was either in Petersburg or some provincial corps. Damn! if that's true, how can I find Zinaida now?"

Osokin walks back down the street. A sledge overtakes him and stops at the gate of the Krutitskys' house. A little girl and a lady wearing a fur cape get out of the sledge. While the lady is settling with the driver, Osokin walks past and looks at the little girl.

"Is it Zinaida or not? I don't think so, I should surely recognize her. But perhaps it is; in any case, this little girl is like her."

He turns round once more. The lady in the fur cape notices him and looks at him in surprise; Osokin flushes and walks on faster without looking back.

"Damn! how stupid! A schoolboy who stares at a little girl: and it's not her at all. And why should the lady give me such a surprised and questioning look? How absurd it is! People always take things in a stupid way. How could she know why I turned round? How idiotic! Still, I wonder who they were. It's a pity I didn't see the lady properly. Perhaps she was Zinaida's mother, but I don't think so."

He stops at the corner of the street.

Well now, what next? So far I'm behaving like an ordinary schoolboy, and I can't think of anything else to do. It's

* A courtyard porter.

simply silly to walk up and down an empty side-street, and besides it's getting cold. Also, it would be awkward if they noticed me. They would say afterwards: 'We've seen you before. You were always walking up and down our street. Why?' No, I'll go away. Anyhow, I know where they live. What a pity that I may not be able to find Krutitsky."

He turns the corner.

CHAPTER XI
MOTHER

AT HOME. Sunday evening. Osokin and his mother are sitting at the tea table. She is reading; and he is looking at her, thinking that soon she may die. The scenes of her funeral, on a sunny frosty day, rise vividly before him. He feels cold and distressed at the thought of this, and he is frightened and terribly sorry for her.

Osokin's mother puts down her book and looks up at him.

"Have you done your lessons, Vanya?"

This question catches Osokin unawares. He had quite forgotten about lessons. All his thoughts were so far away from anything connected with school. His mother's question seems boring and petty and it irritates him.

"Oh, Mother," he says, "you are always talking about lessons. There's plenty of time yet. I was thinking of something quite different."

She smiles. "I know you were thinking of something different, but it will be unpleasant for you if you go to school tomorrow with your lessons unprepared. If you sit up at night you will not wake in the morning."

Osokin feels that she is right. But he is reluctant to give up his sad thoughts. There is something entrancing about them, while his mother's words remind him of material, ordinary everyday things. Besides he wants to forget that he is a schoolboy and that there are textbooks, lessons and school. He wishes that his mother could understand his thoughts, could understand how sorry he is for her, how much he loves her and how strange it seems to him now that he could ever have resigned himself to her death. He feels that he cannot tell her anything, that all this is too fantastic, and even to himself it appears like one of his usual daydreams.

How can he tell her about the magician, about that former life from which he has returned? How, indeed, convey to her why the very sight of her evokes in him such piercing pity and pain? He would like to find some way, even if indirectly, by which it would be possible to tell her about it all. But his mother's words prevent him from speaking of this and make him think of things he wants to forget.

"Oh, Mother," he says, "you're always talking like that. Well, suppose I don't know my lessons, suppose I don't go to school: is it worth talking about?"

He is irritated and begins to lose the sensation of that other life from which he was looking at this one. It becomes still more difficult to tell his mother what is troubling him, and irritation against her flares up in him and he wants to say something disagreeable, although, at the same time, his pity for her almost approaches physical pain.

"I won't go to school to-morrow," he says.

"Why not?" says his mother, astonished and frightened.

"Oh, I don't know; I've a headache," he answers, using the schoolboy's stock phrase. "I just want to stay at home and think. I can't be among these idiots for so long. If it were not for these stupid punishments I should not be staying at home now. I can't go on like this. They'll shut me up again for two or three weeks."

"Do as you please," says his mother, "but I warn you it will only make things worse for you at school. If you don't go to-morrow they will take it as a challenge on your part—but you must decide for yourself. You know I never interfere in your affairs."

Osokin knows that his mother is right, and this makes him feel still more angry. All this dull reality of life, and the necessity of thinking about it, distracts him from his sad thoughts, from the strange sensation of two lives, from the troubling memories of the past and the future. He does not want to think about the present, he wants to escape from it.

"I won't go to-morrow," he says out of sheer obstinacy, although in his heart he feels how unpleasant this is for his mother, and he realizes that he is going against all his own resolutions to arrange his life in a new way.

"Well, this will be the last time," he says to himself. "I'll think things over to-morrow. I must have a day at home. The school won't run away. Afterwards, I'll set to work."

He wants to go back to his thoughts again.

"Do you know, Mother," he says, "it seems to me that I have lived on the earth before. You were just as you are now, and I was just as I am, and there were many other things too. I often think I could recall everything and tell it to you."

". . . and you loved me then just as little as now and did your best to make things unpleasant for me," says his mother.

At first Osokin does not understand her and looks at her in surprise—so utterly out of harmony are her words with what he is feeling. Then he grasps that she is offended with him for not doing his lessons and not wanting to go to school. It seems both useless and tedious to protest. He feels that at this moment his mother is wholly in this life, and he does not know how to convey to her the sensation of that other life. He grows still more despondent at her failure to understand him.

"You are still talking about all that, Mother," he says. "Well, I will go to school."

He says this reluctantly because in his heart he knows that he will not go. The thought of not going to school is always so strong that it is enough to admit it for a moment and it conquers everything else.

"Of course I want you to go," she says. "You know how they look on your absence at school. The assistant head-master has already told me that they hardly put up with you there as it is."

"Have they sent for you?"

"Why, of course."

Osokin is silent, not knowing what he can say to this. There is every reason why he should go to school next day; but he does not want to, and already knows that he will not go. He tries for some time to find some pretext or justification, but it is unpleasant and boring to think about all that. His own quite different thoughts trouble him. Is there no possible way of conveying them to his mother? It is so necessary, so important that she should understand.

Osokin sits looking at his mother, the most conflicting moods struggling within him. He feels her worry and alarm; and this makes all the memories of his life up to the moment when he went to the magician fade away and seem almost imaginary. His life abroad, Zinaida, the grey house in Arbat where he was living less than a month ago—all this has now become like a dream. Above all he does not want to believe that his mother dies and that he remembers her funeral. To think about that, here in this room, in her presence, seems nightmarish, invented and unreal.

He tries not to think of the past, tries to forget it. In his heart he knows that it has actually happened, but to think of it makes this life altogether unbearable. Three weeks of life at school have made a gap between him and the Osokin who went to the magician. And now the same gap lies between him and his mother.

His thoughts move in a circle, continually stopping at certain particularly painful points.

"I don't believe that mother can die so soon," he thinks as he looks at her. "She is still quite young. Even if it happened then, why should it necessarily be repeated now? Everything ought to be different this time. If I have come back, it's precisely for this purpose. There are things, of course, which do not depend on me; but perhaps by altering my own life I shall alter her life as well. After all, the troubles and vexations she had with me then must have had their effect—she died of heart disease. There will be nothing like that this time."

He longs to tell his mother that he is going to be different, that he is going to work and change his whole life for her sake, so that she may live. He wants to believe that this is possible, that it really will be so. He tries to find some way of conveying this assurance to her, but cannot find the words; he does not know how to approach the subject. He is tormented by the gulf of misunderstanding which lies between him and his mother, a gulf which cannot possibly be bridged.

From his mother his thoughts again wander off to Zinaida. Now he thinks of her without bitterness. The news that she is to marry Minsky has somehow lost its vividness or become merely a threat. Only the good remains: their meetings, going on the river, their talks, the evenings when they used to sit alone together, their dreams, even their arguments—all this will happen again and will be still better without the dark clouds which then obscured it. He will prepare for their new meeting; he will not be in such a helpless position, he will not lose her; and his mother will be alive. She must certainly see Zinaida. He feels that they will like each other.

This thought is particularly disturbing to Osokin. He visualizes quite clearly how he will bring Zinaida here to see his mother. He is conscious of the slight feeling of tension and constraint of the first few minutes which passes off later to be replaced by a wonderful feeling of harmony and assurance as though they had known each other all their lives.

As usual, Osokin begins to picture to himself how things will happen. 'What a dear your mother is,' Zinaida would say, looking at him and smiling as he took her home.

'I told you she was,' he would answer, gently pressing her hand which would give a slight, scarcely perceptible response.

"Will you have some more tea?" asks his mother.

The question makes Osokin start and stare at her in surprise.

For a second he feels ashamed of his sentimental dreams because he realizes that neither Zinaida nor his mother would share in them. Next moment he becomes irritated. Neither Zinaida nor his mother ever understood him or what he feels.

They have both demanded insignificant and external things from him while he strove to give them all that was innermost and deepest in himself.

"Yes, please," he answers mechanically, trying to recover the broken thread of his thoughts.

And so the evening passes.

To his mother, Osokin appears to be unnaturally dreamy, silent and self-absorbed. He answers her in monosyllables; often does not hear her, as though all the time he is thinking of something else. She feels ill at ease with him and sad, and she is afraid for him.

CHAPTER XII
MONDAY

MORNING. The maid calls Osokin at half-past seven. He
wakes up with the uncomfortable feeling of having something
to decide.

"Shall I go to school or not?" Yesterday he did not even
open his books. It is impossible to go with his lessons unprepared. Much better to stay at home for a day or two. At the
bottom of his heart he decided yesterday morning that he
would not go to-day, but he must find some pretext. What a
nuisance having told his mother that he would go.

For a long time he lies in bed instead of getting up. He puts
his watch by the pillow and follows the movement of the
hands. The maid comes in several times. At last, at half-past
eight when he ought to be at school, Osokin gets up. He is
annoyed with himself for staying at home and yet he feels
that nothing could have induced him to go to school. To-day
he wants to think of something pleasant; everything unpleasant, difficult and tedious shall be put off until the day after
to-morrow. To-day he will lie on the sofa, read and think . . .
But something seems to gnaw at his heart; he cannot get rid
of his qualms of conscience and of an uneasy feeling about
himself.

"This is all wrong," he tells himself. "If I have really come
back here to change everything, why am I doing things in the
same old way? No, I must decide firmly in what way and
from what moment everything has to be changed. After all,
perhaps it is a good thing that I've stayed at home. At least
I can think things over quietly. But why do I feel so wretch-

ed? Now that I've done it I ought to be feeling cheerful, otherwise it is just as unpleasant to stay here as to go to school."

At that moment he realizes that he is depressed at the thought of how he is going to face his mother. The worst of it is, she will say nothing. It would be much easier if they discussed it together and tried to see each other's point of view. Then perhaps, in talking with her he might find a way of making her understand what he knows, and what he is thinking about. Unfortunately it will not be like that. She will say nothing—and that is the most unpleasant thing of all.

Osokin feels dissatisfied with himself and disgusted with the whole world.

"Now I remember just such a morning when I didn't go to school," he says to himself. "I remember it led to a great deal of trouble, and in the end my position at school became absolutely unbearable. No, all this must be altered. I shall begin work to-day. I'll send to the school and ask someone to write out what preparation has been set. Then I must have a talk with Mother; I cannot be a boarder. She must arrange for me to be a day-boy."

His imagination quickly draws a picture of himself sitting with his mother in the evening, doing his lessons. A warm, pleasant feeling comes over him and in this mood he leaves the room.

Osokin is having breakfast with his mother. She is hurt and remains silent. He is annoyed because she does not realize that he has seriously decided to begin working and because she still attaches importance to his not having gone to school to-day. He sulks and remains silent. His mother leaves the dining-room without saying a word. Osokin feels injured. There was so much he wanted to tell her but she raises a barrier, somehow, between them. He feels unhappy. When he thinks of school he realizes that his absence to-day will not be passed over without a reckoning. Now he has not the slightest desire to begin to do anything, either to read or to think, and, least of all, to learn his lessons.

He stands by the window for some time, and then walks resolutely towards the door.

"I'll go for a short walk," he says to himself. "Then I'll come back and set to work."

To him it is extraordinarily exciting to see Moscow streets now. To begin with, on a week-day—an unusual time for him —everything looks different; and too, the most familiar places now remind him of the past, of what happened at another time. They are full of strange disturbing memories.

Osokin returns home for lunch.

"A teacher has been here from the school," the maid tells him. "He spoke with the mistress. He was very angry."

Osokin's heart sinks.

"How could I have forgotten that?" he asks himself. "The assistant headmaster must have sent one of the masters. Why, of course! And he didn't even find me at home. I remember this is just what happened. Now the trouble will start. I wonder what mother said to him."

His mother comes in. She looks upset.

"Vanya, a master from your school has been here," she says, "and I didn't even know you were out. I didn't know what to say to him. I tried to invent something—said you had suffered all night with toothache and had probably gone to the dentist, but it all sounded very clumsy. He said that as soon as you came home you were to go at once to the school taking the dentist's certificate with you, otherwise they will send to him themselves. All this is so disagreeable for me. I don't know how to lie. This master cross-examined me like a detective, asked me when you went to bed, when you got up, to which dentist had you gone. Why do you put me in such a position? What are you going to do now?"

Osokin feels sorry for her; he feels penitent and ashamed, and, above all, terrified by the fact that everything is beginning to happen exactly as before, as though the wheel of some terrible machine were slowly turning, a wheel to which he is bound and which he can neither stop nor hold back. Yes, all this happened before. He recalls every small detail—his mother's words, the expression on her face, the frozen window panes—and he does not know what to reply.

"I wanted to talk to you, Mother," he says at last with a kind of chill at his heart, knowing that he is repeating his former words. "I can't go on being a boarder, and I shall not go to school to-day. You will have to go and speak to the headmaster. They must let me be a day-boy. I've been kept in for three Sundays and all this time we have not been out of doors. The masters are too lazy to take the boarders out for walks and they make the bad weather their excuse. Each one thinks only of himself and no one realizes that they all do exactly the same. Tell that to the headmaster. It's a scandal. I can't bear it any more."

"You know, Vanya, that I have always wanted you to live at home myself," says his mother, "but you understand that if you cease to be a boarder you will lose the right of free education at the government expense. You will not be able to claim it again later. Think what would happen to you if I died suddenly. I should like you to stay another year or two as a boarder."

"I don't want to think that you may die," says Osokin. "You are not going to. Why think about it? Perhaps I shall die before you. I can't live at school any longer. I can't stand it. It is better to lose this government scholarship."

They talk for a long time and then his mother goes out. Osokin is left alone.

"This is terrible," he says to himself. "Is it possible that the magician is right? Is it true that I cannot change anything? Up to now, everything has gone like clockwork. It becomes terrifying, but it cannot be like that. I am not a schoolboy. I'm a grown man. Why then can I not deal with the life and affairs of a schoolboy? It's too absurd. I must take myself in hand and make myself work and think about the future. So

far, everything is for the best. I shall be a day-boy. I know
that will be arranged. Then things will be easier. I shall read,
draw and write. I must try not to forget anything. How is my
English?"

He thinks for a long time.

"There are many things I can't remember. I shall tell
Mother that I want to learn English. Buy some kind of English manual and pretend to learn it; I'm sure I shall still be
able to read English. But the main thing is to do my school
work. Not for anything on earth will I stay a second year in
the same form. If I don't stay, it will mean that I shall finish
school. When I pass to the fifth form it will be a sign that I
have begun to change things for the better. I remember I remained in the fourth form before."

CHAPTER XIII
REALITY AND THE FAIRY TALE

A YEAR LATER. The gymnasium at school before lunch. Osokin and Sokoloff are standing by the window looking out towards the courtyard. Osokin is now a day-boy but he has remained in the fourth form and Sokoloff has caught up with him.

"What's this new trouble between you and the Turnip?" asks Sokoloff. "I don't understand what it is all about."

"Oh, nothing particular. They are all idiots. You were not at the geography lesson. Well, I was answering about towns on the Volga. I began from the top and came to Nijni, and I said that this is the town where the Volga falls into the Oka.

"At first he didn't understand, then simply leapt up and shouted at me: 'You don't know what you are saying. You mean where the Oka falls into the Volga.'

" 'No,' I said, 'I mean just what I said—where the Volga falls into the Oka.'

"He shouted, 'Are you mad?'

" 'No,' I said, 'I'm not mad at all.'

" 'Then what do you mean?'

" 'I mean that there is a mistake in our geography books because it is not the Oka that falls into the Volga, but the Volga that falls into the Oka.'

"You know he just opened his mouth and couldn't say anything!

" 'How do you know?' he said at last.

" 'Oh,' I said, 'I've seen it myself. When you stand on the high bank of the Oka, you see that the Volga, with its two flat banks, falls into the Oka which is much bigger than the Volga at this place, and certainly it is the Oka that continues further with one high bank.'

"He became quite crazy; sent for Gustav, then for Zeus, but Zeus didn't come. I think he was still at his lunch."

"They may expel you."

"Oh, quite easily. You cannot imagine how tired I am of all this. I am tired of these boys and of all these idiots."

Sokoloff shrugs his shoulders.

"I don't understand you," he says. "You wanted to be a day-boy. Now you are a day-boy, what more do you want? What the devil is it to you whether the Oka falls into the Volga or the Volga falls into the Oka? You are interested in everything that does not concern you. One day they find your desk full of newspapers. We are interested in politics! Another day they find such books that our pedagogues don't even know which end to begin from. You're damned funny! Do what you like at home, but why drag everything into school? And you do nothing that you ought to do. You learned English in one summer, but in Greek you've had 'unsatisfactory' two years running."

"But don't you understand?" says Osokin. "It bores me. What do I want Greek for? Tell me, what for? If ever I need it, I'll learn it, but why now?"

"Now? So that you can finish school and go to the University," says Sokoloff. "You keep on philosophizing when you ought to take things simply."

"Oh, you're too sensible. I shall be glad when you slip up at last."

"I shan't slip up."

"We'll see about that." Osokin looks at Sokoloff and laughs. He is often amused because he knows what is going to happen.

An assistant master comes up to them.

"Osokin, go to the big hall, the headmaster wants you," he says.

"So they've got you! Good-bye. We shan't see each other again," laughs Sokoloff.

Osokin laughs too, but rather nervously. These explanations with the school authorities are always unpleasant, and there is a heavy score of sins standing against him.

Ten minutes later Osokin runs into Sokoloff in the doorway of the classroom.

"What, still alive?"

"Yes, old Turnip has lost. Zeus was in a rather good mood to-day. Evidently he'd had a good lunch. When I told him that the Volga falls into the Oka, he laughed like a crocodile and said that he never knew that and always thought it was the Caspian Sea. On the whole, he was quite benevolent and rather amused.

"Well, I'm to be kept in school till after five, and of course it's 'for the last time' and all the rest of it; the next time he 'won't even talk to me' and so on."

"Did he say that?"

"Why yes, of course, the fat pig!"

"So you're to be kept in! You know, they say the Inspector of the Educational Circuit is coming. They will show you off to him as an exemplary pupil—knows English, reads Schopenhauer, and is so diligent that he refuses to leave school until six o'clock."

"Then he'll probably come during lessons."

"No, afterwards, they say."

"Well, he can go to hell!"

Osokin goes to his seat.

Second bell. The French teacher comes in. This is one of Osokin's favorite lessons. He is in a privileged position because he knows enough French not to have to bother about the lessons. He need pay no attention to what is going on, and can think his own thoughts. The Frenchman does not worry him and only occasionally—in fact very rarely—calls him to his desk, chats with him in French for a few minutes and gives him full marks. The Frenchman is the only teacher who speaks to him as to a grown-up, and Osokin always feels inwardly grateful to him. When they meet in the street, the

Frenchman always stops to shake hands and talk. "The only decent man here," thinks Osokin looking at him.

Osokin opens the famous 'Margot'—the French manual on which many generations of Russian boys have forgotten what little they may have known of French before going to school—and becomes engrossed in his thoughts.

"I understand everything less and less," he says to himself. "If I've come back here from another life, and if all I see here is real, then where is Zinaida, and where are all the others? Some are here, but does it mean that they go on living there at the same time? If this is so, it means that we not only live in one time and in one place, but that we live in different times and in different places simultaneously. That alone is enough to drive one mad. How can one find out the truth? Has it happened or not? No, it's better not to think about it. I'll read. How can I live without reading? It is the only way to escape from my thoughts."

He opens an English book under the desk. It is Stevenson's 'Fables.'

"Yes, here's the tale," he says to himself. "'The Song of the Morrow.' How can the title be translated? Well, there is no escape from thoughts after all, so I'll at least try to make some sense out of this tale."

Osokin reads for a long time trying to fathom the meaning of Stevenson's strange fable. At last he shuts the book and sits gazing into space, almost without thought. In this tale there is some hidden inner meaning of which he is vaguely conscious . . . With it are connected so many strange and incomprehensible memories.

CHAPTER XIV
PUNISHED

THE SAME DAY after lessons. An empty classroom. Osokin is sitting with a book at a desk by the window. It is growing dark.

Osokin closes the book, looks straight in front of him for some time, then glances at the lamp.

"Evidently they are not going to give me a light," he thinks. "Very well, I'll have to sit in the dark, but how stupid all this is. God, how stupid it is! And what does life itself actually mean if I cannot alter anything? It is only a wound-up clock. What then is the sense of anything? What sense is there in my life, in my sitting here in school? Of course I cannot force myself to be a schoolboy. Of course I'm bored without people, without life. I cling to books in order not to lose myself in these surroundings. I feel that with these boys I often become a boy myself. I am becoming ridiculous in my own eyes. I am like a man who, finding himself obliged to live in a distant province, tries to maintain an inner connection with the capital so as not to become provincial: he subscribes to papers and magazines which are really quite useless and even ludicrous in his provincial life, and he likes to think about things which perhaps had meaning in Moscow or in Petersburg but have no meaning at all where he is. In any case, all this is rather funny. I have a special interest in reading the newspapers because I know what is going to happen. Only it's a pity I've forgotten so much. After all, the magician was right. Not only can I alter nothing, but I am beginning to forget a great deal. It's strange how quickly some impressions disappear from memory. They are preserved in the memory solely through constant repetition. If repetition

STRANGE LIFE OF IVAN OSOKIN

stops, they disappear. I have a regular kaleidoscope of faces and events in my memory, but I've forgotten almost all names. I have tried to find Zinaida, but I've failed. To keep on walking past their house is absurd. I found the girls' school where she should be now. I waited there two Saturdays, but how can I recognize anyone? The girls come together in a crowd. They laugh. And certainly I must look funny standing there as though I were a Lycée boy. Although I liked two of the girls, neither of them could have been Zinaida, they were both older than she would be. Krutitsky is not in any cadet corps here. So it means he is not in Moscow, and I can meet him only in the Military School. But by then Zinaida will already have gone abroad and will not return for six or seven years. Very well, it is inevitable. I must either find her abroad or wait here, but I must not be in the same helpless position when I do meet her. By that time I may already have taken my University degree. There will be no need to go to the Military School, and everything will be quite different. The dreadful thing is, I do nothing to achieve this . . . How could it have happened that I was left for a second year in the same form? To lose a year! Four and a half more years inside these walls! I don't know, but it seems to me, I shall never be able to stand it. The chief thing is that now I've lost every aim and am simply bored with knowing all that I know; and the worst of it is that when I was at school before I was equally bored, because then too I knew everything. This is the most awful thought. It seems to me that everything repeats itself, not once or twice, but scores of times, like the 'Blue Danube' on a barrel organ. And I know it all by heart.

"And sometimes I think exactly the opposite—that nothing has happened before, that I have imagined it all, that there was no magician, no Zinaida, no other life. But where I could have got it all from—and many other things—I don't know. Only one thing is certain in all this. I often want to smash my head against the wall from sheer boredom!"

CHAPTER XV
BOREDOM

OSOKIN GETS UP from the desk and walks up and down the half-dark classroom. Then he goes to the big glass door that leads to the corridor and tries the handle. The door is not locked.

"They've forgotten to lock it," he says to himself. "Is there nothing I can do? It's so awfully dull. I've still a whole hour to sit here."

He hears a noise, and then footsteps hurrying along the corridor.

"Probably they are expecting the great man, or perhaps he has arrived," Osokin says to himself. He opens the door a little and looks out. "There's no one there. Well, let's go and reconnoiter."

He steps quietly into the corridor. All is still. Glancing through the glass doors of the empty classrooms as he goes along, Osokin reaches the library or reception room where, in his dream, he saw the unknown girl. The room is brilliantly lit. He looks cautiously round the edge of the door. There is no one there.

"Damn!" he says. "His Excellency will be going through here. Shall I write something on the wall? 'Welcome your Excellency' with one or two mistakes? That would be a good idea. What a pity there's no chalk."

He thinks.

"But there's something still better I can do." He puts his hand into his pocket and takes out a pair of blue spectacles. Facing him, on a bracket over the door leading to the big hall, stands a plaster bust of Caesar.

"I'll put the blue spectacles on Caesar. That's bound to be noticed."

Osokin runs on tiptoe to the other end of the library, brings a chair, climbs on it and puts the blue spectacles on Caesar's nose. The spectacles fit beautifully and Caesar acquires a scholarly air.

Osokin carries the chair back to its place and runs into the corridor. Now he no longer wants to go back to the empty classroom; he wants to devise something else. He tries the doors of the classrooms along the corridor one after another. One proves to be unlocked. Osokin looks all around him, then slips inside and gropes about until he finds a piece of chalk behind a blackboard. He runs back to the library, and on the wall, just underneath the 'golden tablets' on which the names of head boys are inscribed, he writes in plain round letters, unlike his own, and misspelling all the words: 'Welcome your Excellency!' Then he draws an ugly face with a gaping mouth and astonished eyes, and, shaking with laughter, runs back to his own classroom.

There he sits down on the window sill and looks into the street where the lamps are already lit.

"What the devil drives me to do all these stupid things?" he asks himself. "Now they will start an inquiry and of course they will think of me first. The worst of it is, I remember quite clearly that I did this very same thing before and I was expelled for it. Now, why did I do it? Of course it is tedious here but that's what school is for. Can these idiots understand a joke? For them I'm an ordinary schoolboy. Of course they will guess I did it. If only I could lock myself in somehow..."

He goes to the door and tries the handle. Then he looks at his watch. "Another half-hour to wait. If only I could get away."

He walks up and down. After five minutes he stops at the window again and looks into the street.

"Well, the spectacles wouldn't matter so much," he says, "but they won't forgive me for the misspelled 'Excellency' and the face on the wall. The spectacles too. That is disrespectful and all the rest of it. Well, of course I'll deny any knowledge of anything. '*I am not I, and the horse is not mine, and I am not the driver . . .*' but unfortunately the assistant headmaster has a way of nosing me out. Often nothing points to me, but he simply says: 'Call Osokin' and that is all. It will be like that now—no need even to call me when it comes out that I was sitting in a classroom nearby: the whole thing will be perfectly clear. Damn! Perhaps I had better go and rub it out? No, it's not worth while. I might get into a worse mess."

He looks at his watch.

"Fifteen minutes more. I wonder if I could lock myself in?"

He goes to the door again and examines the lock. There are footsteps in the corridor; Osokin jumps away from the door and again goes to the window. Time passes slowly. He looks at his watch every minute.

At last 'Cockroach,' the class servant, comes to the door with a bunch of keys. He fumbles for a long time picking out a key; tries to unlock the door, shakes his head, takes another key. Finally he gives the door a tug and it opens.

"What's this?" he asks. "Was it unlocked?"

"No, locked," answers Osokin, coming up to the door. "You unlocked it with the first key."

"Well, you can go," says the Cockroach. "Khrenytch told me to let you out."

"Well, Cockroach," says Osokin, "here's twenty kopecks for you."

The Cockroach is very pleased and gives Osokin a friendly pat on the back.

"Cockroach will be on my side," says Osokin to himself, "but the show will soon begin, so now is the time to save my skin."

He runs downstairs and through the gymnasium to the hall which is lit with unusual brilliance in readiness for the arrival of His Excellency.

CHAPTER XVI
ZEUS

THE FOLLOWING MORNING at school. Osokin, from the moment he enters the school, feels something unusual in the air. The boys are all standing about in groups and whispering. On the landing Osokin runs into Sokoloff.

"Well, brother," says Sokoloff, "if it's your doing, then well done! But this time it'll be all up with you."

"What do you mean?"

"Oh, don't pretend to be innocent. You know quite well."

"I don't," says Osokin. "As soon as I came in I felt that something had happened, but what is it?"

"Well, it's like this. Yesterday the Circuit Inspector was due to arrive. You know they say he's had a grudge against Zeus for a long time. He arrived after five and it seems that someone had put spectacles on Caesar—you know, over the door in the reception room—and had written on the wall 'Your Excellency is a fool' or something of that sort. Well, I bet you know more about it than any of us. There was a row. The Inspector was furious—or pretended to be. He hissed at Zeus that he couldn't keep the school in order and without another word turned and went away. Now there's an inquiry going on. Zeus has ordered all the servants on this floor to be dismissed: Cockroach, who was on duty, Vassily and the Cossack. They all put it on you. You were sitting alone in a classroom at the time and you went away just before the Inspector's arrival. There! They are calling for you."

"Osokin to the headmaster! Osokin! Osokin!" voices can be heard shouting in the corridor.

Osokin walks through the crowd of schoolboys. They all look at him with curiosity. He goes along the corridor, through the library where the bust of Caesar stands, and into the big hall.

At the far end of the big hall, with its life-size portraits of the Tsars in heavy gold frames, the headmaster, Zeus; the assistant headmaster, Gustav Lukitch—and several teachers are seated at a long table covered with a green cloth. Three servants, two assistant masters and Khrenytch, alias Turnip, the master who was on duty the day before, are standing near.

Osokin walks up to the table. The headmaster is very angry. Osokin glances at the servants. Two of them, and especially Cockroach, look at him with suspicion and hostility. Vassily, his particular friend, tries not to look at him. At first the headmaster cannot speak for fury and simply snorts. At last he finds his breath and begins, avoiding Osokin's eye. Osokin feels that Zeus is particularly displeased with himself because yesterday he laughed when he heard about the Volga and the Oka.

"Were you kept in till five o'clock in a classroom yesterday after lessons?"

"Yes," says Osokin.

"Did you leave the room?"

"No."

"Did you go into the library?"

"No."

"You lie, you scoundrel!" The headmaster turns purple in the face and bangs his fist on the table.

Osokin flushes and takes a step towards him. Their eyes meet. Something dangerous flashes across Osokin's face and the headmaster looks away.

Osokin wants to shout something rude and insulting at him to pay him back for his offensive language and for all that he has endured at the school; for all the boredom, all the lack of understanding; but his voice catches, his lower lip trembles, and for a few seconds he is unable to say anything.

Recovering his breath, the headmaster, without looking at Osokin, says:

"Which man was on duty?"

"Ivanoff," says the assistant headmaster, and Cockroach comes to attention.

"Did you lock the door of the classroom where Osokin was sitting?" asks the headmaster.

"Can't say, your Excellency, who locked it. I was in the garden," says Cockroach. "When I came back to open it, it wasn't locked. Must have opened it himself for sure."

Cockroach looks spitefully at Osokin. This look gives Osokin an unpleasant feeling. He feels sorry for Cockroach and the other two men, but somewhat disgusted at the thought that he could ever have joked and talked with him in a friendly way.

"How do you mean, 'opened it himself'?" asks the head-master.

"Must have broken the lock, your Excellency. I came to unlock it and not one key would turn. I pull the door, it opens. I say to him: 'You're not locked in, Osokin?' and he says: 'Yes, I am locked in. Don't say anything'; and gives me twenty kopecks. Here!"

Sweating with the strain, Cockroach thrusts his hand into his pocket and produces a twenty-kopeck coin.

Everyone looks at the coin and then at Osokin.

Osokin is both disgusted and amused.

He realizes that this twenty-kopeck coin is the strongest evidence against him. And although he knows that what happened was quite different, he feels that it is useless to protest. He has had far too good a schoolboy training to do this. It is considered permissible to try to prove oneself inno-cent and for that purpose to lie as much as is necessary, but only when there is a chance of succeeding and of making one's accuser look foolish. If there is no such possibility, the school-boy's code demands a stoic silence no matter whether the accusation is just or unjust.

At the same time Osokin has a growing desire to laugh. Suddenly he feels very remote from all this. He becomes conscious of himself as a grown-up man; he feels that what is happening here is not happening to him. His indignation disappears completely and he now coldly observes the proceedings as an onlooker.

"Is the lock really broken?" the headmaster asks the assistant headmaster.

"The lock won't work," says the latter. "Something must have been put into it."

"Enough!" says the headmaster. He snorts again for a second or two.

"Well then," he says at last, addressing Osokin, "you can exercise your talents elsewhere. We have no need here for lockpickers, liars and scoundrels. You can let the men stay on," he says aside to the assistant headmaster. "They must not suffer because of this . . ."

"I think there are enough of us here for the Council," he says looking round.

Then he addresses one of the assistant masters. "Take him to the reception room and wait with him. When I send for you, you will bring him here."

Osokin walks with the assistant master known as 'the Violin' to the reception room. As he passes he sees the Cockroach still standing with the twenty-kopeck coin in his open palm, and he feels so amused that he only restrains himself with an effort from laughing aloud. They come to the reception room and there they sit and wait. Osokin's brain is somewhat dulled and he does not want to think of anything.

After five or ten minutes, another assistant master, a little man with a red beard, known as 'Prophet Elias,' opens the door from the big hall and nods to 'the Violin.'

They go to the big hall.

The headmaster takes a large official-looking sheet of paper from the table in front of him, coughs twice and then reads aloud without looking at Osokin.

"By the decision of the Masters' Council, the pupil of the Fourth Form, Ivan Osokin, is excluded from the number of pupils of the Second Moscow Gymnasium with a conduct mark of three."

The headmaster puts the sheet on the table, then rises, walks to the desk with an air of importance and takes up a report book.

Osokin realizes that all is over for him here. For a moment he is again seized with anger against the stupid people who are deciding his fate, but, as if in answer to this, he is pierced by the cold sensation that it has all happened before, and happened in exactly the same way. He feels himself disappearing in this sensation. *He is not!* He does not exist! Something is happening around him but not to him; therefore, all this is completely and absolutely of no account to him. He can no more be troubled by it than he can be troubled by some event of Roman history.

All these people, the headmaster, the assistant headmaster, Cockroach, think that this is actually happening now. They do not understand that everything has already been and that nothing therefore exists.

Osokin cannot explain to himself why, if this has happened before, it means that it does not exist now. He feels that it is so, and he feels that nothing concerns him any more.

CHAPTER XVII
THE SCHOOL INFIRMARY

'THE VIOLIN' touches Osokin on the shoulder and they walk out of the hall.

"What's to happen to me now?" Osokin asks, with a grin. "May I go home?"

"No," answers the assistant master. "Your mother will be sent for and she will take you away."

He walks with Osokin, through all the corridors and staircases to the school infirmary.

The infirmary consists of three small rooms, set apart on the ground floor, with a separate entrance from the courtyard. Two boys from the first form, dressed in blue dressing gowns are there, and a fat youth in spectacles from the seventh form, whom Osokin dislikes. The boys suspect him of having syphilis and he spends almost all his time in the infirmary.

The assistant master leaves Osokin and goes away.

Osokin sits by the window and looks out into the street.

The sensation of indifference to himself and to everything else in the world disappears. He feels himself a schoolboy at whom the headmaster has just been shouting—a schoolboy who has just been expelled from school.

"What have you been up to, Osokin?" asks the youth in spectacles.

"Oh, nothing in particular," answers Osokin, turning away. The boy stands near him, for a time obviously not knowing what to say, then goes into another room.

Time passes slowly. The first form boys are playing dominoes in the next room. Osokin sits looking out of the window. He feels so sick at heart that he is even afraid to think.

"What does it mean?" he says to himself. "I know that it was necessary for me to finish school so that I could do everything as I wanted. But what has come of it? The same thing over again. Now I know that then, too, I sat in the same way by the window and thought exactly what I am thinking at this moment: here I am expelled from school. So it means that everything repeats itself without change. Then what was the use of returning? It means I shall never go to the University in the normal way. Poor Mother! She wanted that so much. What a damnable thing to do to her. Her heart is not so strong. Now they will drag her here and tell her all sorts of horrible things about me and she will feel that I am almost ruined. In any case, all this means a great deal to her. Afterwards, of course, things will come right somehow. I shall work for matriculation. It does not follow that I shall have to go to the Military School. But it is now, *now* that is so bad. Poor Mother, these idiots will torture her to death. What I cannot understand is why I did it; for I remember the whole business of the spectacles and Caesar perfectly well. To be quite honest with myself, I knew everything from the beginning to end; I knew I should be caught. I even knew I should be accused of breaking the lock—and yet I've done exactly what I did before. Why the devil did I want to play with Caesar or the Circuit Inspector? The most curious thing of all is that *then*, the other time, I also knew everything and afterwards sat here just like this and accused myself of having done it all in spite of the fact that I knew beforehand what the result would be. I remember this quite clearly now. What will happen next? Is it possible that everything will *go on* in the same way as before? No, that would be horrible! It is impossible to believe that. I must find something to hold on to. It cannot continue like this. I must not give way to these thoughts. Yes, it is all bad, very bad, but after all, there must be some way out. Evidently I could not alter anything at school. Probably everything had been spoiled beforehand. Here my hands were tied, but now I shall be free. I shall work,

I shall read. It is much better so, after all. I shall prepare for matriculation far more quickly at home. In two years I can be at the University. Only I must persuade Mother not to be too disappointed. I must make her understand that school was only a hindrance to me. That is probably the reason why everything may be for the best. I can begin now with a clean sheet and write on it whatever I like."

Osokin, sitting motionless by the window, begins to feel cold and hungry. Sounds are heard overhead.

"The second break," thinks Osokin.

Then the noise dies down; evidently lessons have begun. The time drags on incredibly slowly. At last lunch is brought to the infirmary. The dining-hall attendant who has brought the food chats with the infirmary attendant. The seventh-form boy in spectacles goes up to them and Osokin can hear that they are talking about him. A wave of anger and disgust with all of them sweeps over him. He is sick of sitting here; he is bored and cold, he wants to eat and wants to smoke. But at the same time he wants this to last as long as possible so that his mother shall not arrive too soon.

Lunch is over. There is a clatter of plates. The trays are cleared away. The noise begins again upstairs. Long break. Time drags on endlessly. At last everything is quiet once more. Osokin begins to hope that his mother will not come. It will make everything much easier. He will then be sent home with an assistant master.

"But after the fourth lesson I shall try to go out with the day-boys," he thinks. "The porters, of course, have been told not to let me out, but it might be possible to slip through."

Osokin goes into the next room. The attendant is not there. It would be possible to walk out, but he must wait for a break. He sits down by the window again.

Now he has not the slightest desire to think about school and about being expelled. His thoughts wander to other far more pleasant subjects. Osokin thinks of the summer, of how he will buy a gun and go out shooting. One scene after another comes up and passes before him: a wooded lake, a marsh with silver birches . . . Then he looks round and is almost amused at having taken his expulsion from school so calmly.

"I believe I really did know that this was going to happen and that is why I am not surprised," he says to himself.

At last, when Osokin least expects it, a door bangs in the adjoining room and the assistant master comes in with his mother. The first form boys stand at the door and gaze at her with curiosity. The fat boarder opens his door and also looks on curiously.

Osokin sees that his mother is deeply distressed, and his heart sinks. That calm with which he was so pleased a moment ago, now appears to him as the most callous selfishness. His plans for matriculation and going to the University fall to the ground, and nothing remains except the naked and ugly truth: he is expelled from school. And he knows what that means to his mother.

"What is all this, Vanya?" she asks.

He makes no reply but glances towards the assistant master.

"Why do you ask me in front of this ape? What can I say?" he says in his mind. But really he looks as though he is silent because he is ashamed.

"Let's go," he says aloud. "I will tell you everything. It was all quite different."

They leave the infirmary and go through the corridor and the empty gymnasium to the hall. Suddenly Osokin feels that after all he is fond of the school and that he is sorry to be leaving, never to return. It is stupid and annoying to realize that he has been expelled. He sees that his mother is very depressed, and he feels most uncomfortable.

In the hall his mother is nervous. For a long time she cannot find her gloves. She looks for her purse and gives the porter a much bigger tip than is necessary.

Osokin is terribly sorry for her and at the same time annoyed with her for coming. It would have been far better if she had left him to get out of this alone.

They go into the street.

"What are you doing to me, Vanya?" she says. "Why do you subject me to such humiliation, and what are you doing to yourself?" Her voice fails her. Osokin feels that she is going to burst into tears.

"Let's go home, Mother," he says. "I will tell you everything there." He wants to add that everything will be all right, but after one glance at his mother's face, he is silent.

They get into a sledge and drive off. Osokin does not speak on the way home and only occasionally looks at his mother. She too is silent.

"There is one thing I want to know," thinks Osokin. "*Why, knowing all that was going to happen,* have I acted as I have done? Why did I not act differently? And, if I couldn't, why does it often seem to me that everything depends entirely on myself?"

He thinks intently.

"A rabbit, when a snake looks at it, probably reasons in exactly the same way as I do," he says to himself. "Why does it not run away? It is quite free, and it *knows* what is going to happen: the snake will swallow it if it doesn't escape. It wants to run away, but instead of that it moves nearer and nearer to the snake. Each moment, as it moves nearer to the snake's jaws, it probably wonders why it is doing it. But the chief point is: why does the rabbit do this, knowing all the time exactly what the end will be? Perhaps the rabbit thinks there will still be a possibility of escape.

"Does all this mean that I must admit I am beaten? No, I am not beaten. I shall try to find Zinaida now."

By this time, Osokin has developed the habit of observing his own thoughts and of looking at himself from outside, and he suspects that "trying to find Zinaida" will be merely a pretext for not staying at home—which means not doing any work—and that ultimately nothing will come of his fine intentions. He feels thoroughly disgusted with himself.

Were he alone, Osokin could easily restore his spirits by making himself dream about something pleasant. But his mother's presence is a living reminder and a living reproach that forces him all the time to see the real truth of life and the results to which all his good intentions have led. At the same time he is very tired of thinking in a minor key—as he involuntarily puts it to himself—and his thoughts wander off by themselves in more pleasant directions . . . He dislikes remaining in an unpleasant mood for long.

CHAPTER XVIII
AT HOME

OSOKIN AND HIS MOTHER reach home and go into her room.

"Well, what does all this mean?" she asks. "Which lock did you break, and what other dreadful things have you done? The headmaster spoke about you as though you were a criminal. They would not even allow me to take you away at my own request so that you would have the right to go to another school. Now you cannot because you are expelled by the decision of the Council." She wipes her eyes with her handkerchief. "I don't know what you are going to do."

"That's all nonsense, Mother," says Osokin. "I didn't break any lock. I was left in an empty classroom after lessons; there was not even a light, and I became terribly bored. You simply cannot imagine how boring it was there. I tried the door and it wasn't locked. Perhaps the lock really was broken, I don't know. I walked down the corridor and came to the waiting-room—you know, where the big library is. They were expecting the Circuit Inspector yesterday. Then . . ." Osokin stops. "You see, there's a bust of Caesar there. Well, I put blue spectacles on it."

"What blue spectacles?"

"Just ordinary spectacles. I had a pair I bought at Soukharevka once. I don't know why. Well, I put the spectacles on Caesar. They made him look awfully funny, just like a German professor. And then I wrote on the wall in chalk: 'Welcome, your Excellency!' with five mistakes in the spelling."

"And is that all?"

"That's all. I drew an ugly face on the wall too."

Osokin's mother wants to laugh, but at the same time she feels very disheartened. What she dreaded most has happened. Vanya will be left without education. The future seems so dark. And this has happened so unexpectedly. It had seemed to her of late that he had become more used to school. She is annoyed with him, but she is much more indignant with the school authorities. She looks at her son. He is constantly thinking about something and he is obviously suffering too. She is deeply grieved and wounded for his sake. She is sorry for him and sorry for all her shattered hopes. But she too wants to believe in a brighter future. In any case, he has done nothing wrong—foolish maybe, but nothing really bad. He is incapable of it, of this she is certain. And with this thought, a great weight falls from her.

"What are you going to do now?" she asks.

"Oh, Mother," says Osokin, "everything will be much better now. I am going to prepare for matriculation and I shall go to the University much sooner than I should have done from school. You saw how I learned English: it will be the same with other things. You'll see. At school, I was only wasting time."

Osokin's mother becomes sad again.

"You will need a tutor to help you," she says.

Osokin starts. She had said this *then*, in exactly the same voice, with the same uncertainty and helplessness. He remembers it.

"I will work Mother, I will," he says. "Forgive me for what has happened. I will do everything, you'll see."

CHAPTER XIX
TANECHKA

EIGHTEEN MONTHS LATER. Osokin's mother is dead. He is living with his uncle, a rich landowner, in a big country house in Middle Russia.

The veranda opens on to the garden. A long avenue of lime trees. Osokin, in top boots, a white Russian shirt with a leather belt, a white cap, and with a Cossack whip hanging from his wrist, is walking up and down on the veranda waiting for his horse.

"Outwardly everything is turning out very well," he says to himself, stopping and looking at the garden, "but all the time something oppresses me. I cannot reconcile myself to the thought that Mother is dead. I can't, and I don't want to. It's six months ago now, but to me it seems like yesterday. I know I shall always feel like this. And I know it's all my fault. Mother was taken ill soon after I was expelled from school and she never fully recovered afterwards. I know it. And the worst of it is, I knew it all before."

He stands thinking.

"Whether all that about meeting the magician was a dream or not, I don't know," he says to himself, "but for me the future has a taste of the past. I know that everything that will happen to me has already happened before, so I have no interest in the future. I feel that it holds nothing but traps and pitfalls. It seems to me that I see them all beforehand, but now that Mother is dead I no longer care. I don't even want anything good for myself."

He walks up and down near the veranda again.

"I feel a little uneasy here," he says, looking round. "Uncle is a nice man, and I see that he is really well disposed towards me, but I have no confidence in the future. I feel that there is going to be trouble between us. I'm constantly on my guard, constantly expecting something. And because of this uneasiness and because of I don't know what, I do nothing. It's eighteen months since I left school and I am still thinking about starting work. I have read plenty of books during this time; I've learned Italian—I can read Dante— I've done some mathematics, but Latin and Greek—I believe I've forgotten how to read Greek. I can't force myself to begin. I shall have to take my examination in modern school. Even that is awfully difficult because of small things. In the syllabus there's so much that is dull and unnecessary— divinity, geography and so forth; and with this examination, without Latin and Greek, I shall not be able to go to the University. But if I pass an examination I know that Uncle will make it possible for me to go abroad to study. Yet I'm so indifferent now to everything that I hardly know whether I want it or not."

Tanechka, his uncle's ward and housekeeper, comes out on the veranda. She is a tall, good-looking girl of Russian type, with a thick plait, rosy cheeks and large dark eyes. She is a little over twenty. She has been to a girls' school in a provincial town and likes to wear Russian peasant dress and to walk about barefoot. The servants say that she has got round the old man.

Tanechka steals up behind Osokin and claps her hands above his head. Osokin turns round quickly and catches her by the arms.

"Oh, Tanechka, how you frightened me!"

"Let me go, you horrid thing! You'll break my arms."

"I won't let you go."

Osokin draws her nearer still. His face is quite close to hers. He looks into her eyes, he sees, so close to him, her slightly parted lips and her small white teeth. He feels the contact of her breasts, her shoulders, her whole body. Suddenly, for a moment, Tanechka stops resisting, and her body becomes soft and tender. Her laughing eyes close and her warm lips, firm and full and smelling of strawberries, are pressed to his. Thousands of electric sparks run through Osokin's body. He is overwhelmed with a joyful surprise and an extraordinarily warm feeling for Tanechka. He wants to press her still closer to him, wants to kiss her, wants to ask why, how has she become like this? But Tanechka has already escaped from his arms and is standing at the other end of the veranda.

"Look! They are bringing White Legs," she says, as though nothing had happened. But she looks at Osokin and smiles, and in her eyes there is a new expression.

A groom leads a saddled horse up to the veranda. It is a sturdy bay mare with white legs, a rather short neck and strangely expressive and lively eyes. She looks very trim with a high Cossack saddle and Caucasian silver stirrups.

Osokin is now reluctant to go. Tanechka is still on the veranda, leaning against the balustrade. Osokin feels that if he were to put his arms round her and press her to him again her body would once more become yielding and tender. This sensation troubles him and draws him to her.

Tanechka assumes an air of innocence and says: "Are you going far, Ivan Petrovitch?"

"To Orehovo for newspapers, Tatyana Nikanorovna," answers Osokin in the same tone, making a low bow.

Tanechka raises her hand as if threatening to hit him, then turns and runs from the veranda into the house.

"Come back in time for dinner," she calls. "I've picked lots of strawberries."

Osokin runs down the veranda steps, tests the saddle girths and strokes the mare's white face down to her warm soft nostrils. White Legs dances a little and rubs her head against his shoulder. Then he takes up the reins, lays a hand on the pommel, puts his foot in the stirrup and lifts himself lightly into the saddle.

"Good-bye!" Tanechka calls to him from a window upstairs. "Don't forget me. Write!"

The groom smiles broadly. Osokin turns White Legs sharply round and breaks at once into a brisk trot down the avenue keeping his legs well back and almost standing in the stirrups.

The strong, resilient movement of the horse under him, the warm wind smelling of flowering limes and the sensation of Tanechka in his whole body carry Osokin away from any thoughts.

The trees flash swiftly by and the thud of hoofs on the soft road sounds wonderfully pleasant. White Legs stretches her neck, pulling at the reins, and goes faster and faster in a swinging trot. Osokin presses his feet more firmly into the stirrups and, with a particularly joyful feeling in his heart, keeps quick time with the movement of the horse.

"Darling," he says, stroking White Legs' neck, and without knowing whether he means Tanechka or White Legs. Tanechka's lips are again quite close to his, and the high, firm breast beneath the white smock is warmly, tenderly and trustfully pressed against him. He even feels slightly dizzy, and tightens his grip on the reins.

"Dear Tanechka!" he says. "How wonderfully good it all is! But that means she felt the same thing as I did. Can that really be true? Yes, yes, it must be. That is why she became so . . ." At that moment a black cloud again rises from some deep place within him.

"Why," he asks, "why is everything so beautiful from one side and so terrible from another? Why is Mother not here? If I knew she were alive, how I should enjoy everything—this road, and the wood, and White Legs and Tanechka. Now I don't want anything. Yesterday I remembered an amusing story. I wanted so much to tell it to Mother, the one person who would have understood it properly. But she is not here and I don't know why she is not here or where she is or what it all means. If it were possible, there is one thing only I should like—to bring back last summer. Why is it not possible?"

He does not realize himself why this thought makes him feel cold and frightened; it is as though he had suddenly touched a most painful spot that he had decided not to touch, or had roused a whole army of ghosts that might at any moment close in upon his soul from all sides. And, in an attempt to get away from himself, he lets White Legs go down the hill, at full gallop, as only Cossack horses can. Then, standing in the stirrups, he trots across a small bridge which shakes under the clattering hoofs, and swiftly climbs the hill, leaning forward in the saddle. Then, raising clouds of dust, he gallops like one pursued, along the old unpaved highroad, a hundred yards wide and bordered with tall silver birches.

An hour and a half later, Osokin returns at a walking pace on a heavily sweating horse. Lost in thought, and sitting slightly sideways in the saddle, he rides out of the wood into a large clearing beyond which the copse adjoining the garden begins.

He now thinks of nothing but Tanechka. Everything else has receded into the background. Tanechka, with her skirt lifted above shapely legs in striped stockings and tiny red shoes, walking carefully through the wet grass; Tanechka, as he once caught sight of her in the early morning, with bare shoulders and half-covered breast, leaning out of the window to count the call of the cuckoo ... And again, the touch of her firm lips and her body becoming tender and soft in his arms.

All these sensations and pictures make Osokin feel happy and light-hearted, but at the same time he wants to behave sensibly.

"Tanechka is a darling," he says to himself, "but I must watch myself carefully so as not to spoil everything. What they say about her and Uncle is nonsense; all the same, I feel that my relationship to him might be spoiled because of Tanechka. If he notices anything, he will consider it his duty to protect her from me, and that is stupid. I don't want anything. Tanechka is part of nature, like this field, or the wood, or the river. I never imagined that the feeling of woman was so much like the feeling of nature. But I must keep myself in hand."

With a touch of the whip he urges his horse into a trot and, crossing the clearing, rides through the copse towards the house.

Tanechka is on the veranda hulling some strawberries for jam, and when Osokin catches sight of her an unaccountably cheerful mood takes possession of him. He wants to chat with her, to laugh and to amuse her. If he were not afraid of his Uncle, he would ride on to the veranda and make White Legs kneel before Tanechka. The head groom had shown him some time ago that White Legs has been specially trained and knows some circus tricks.

"Tanechka, what lots of mushrooms I've seen!" cries Osokin, springing from the saddle.

"Where, where?"

Tanechka runs up to the veranda balustrade.

"Mostly by the Zuevo swamp. Let's go after dinner. I'll show you."

Tanechka throws back her plait and frowns.

"All right," she says. "But it's not going to rain, is it?"

"It doesn't look like it."

"Very well. And now dinner is ready. Come along quickly."

Osokin and Tanechka are walking in a wood. They have a big black dog called Polkan with them. Osokin is carrying two baskets full of mushrooms. They come to a shallow forest stream. All round are old pine trees, and green alder bushes on the banks of the stream.

It is now nearly four hours since they left home, and Osokin is completely in love with Tanechka. They have been talking without stopping. Osokin has told Tanechka about the school, imitating all the masters, and about the French Exhibition in Moscow, and about Paris—he has never been there, although he fancies that he has, because he can see it clearly in his mind. Tanechka has told him about the admirers she has had in the district town, and about the theatre which she has twice visited. And all the time Osokin discovers fresh attraction in her. She laughed so infectiously when he told her about Caesar in blue spectacles. She has a rounded sunburnt neck, silky eyelashes and thick eyebrows. She is supple and strong—"like a nice young cat," Osokin thinks to himself. He is afraid of looking at her too much and often looks away. It seems to him that his glance may convey to her all he is thinking and feeling. He catches fire from his own thoughts. Tanechka often looks at him, and it seems to him that once or twice she has looked at him with some astonishment, as though she had expected something different from him.

"We must cross to the other side," cries Tanechka, running down to the stream. "Let's look for a ford."

She sits down on the grass by the water and quickly pulls off her small shoes and sand colored stockings.

When Osokin comes up to her, she is standing on the sand gathering up the skirt of her *sarafan*, and Osokin sees her white rounded legs with their slim ankles and small feet; and it pleases him that Tanechka does not pay the slightest attention to him. Holding up her dress with one hand and balancing herself with the other, she walks carefully into the water.

"Oh, what sharp stones!" she cries. "But how warm the water is! I am going to bathe. Only, don't you dare to look at me, Go behind there and don't come back until I call you."

Osokin walks over the knoll and comes down again to the stream which curves at this point.

His heart is thumping and he is conscious of an unusually pleasant excitement. A slight shiver runs through his whole body as though he were stepping into cold water; he feels gay and wants to laugh.

He lies down on his back by the water and lights a cigarette.

"Hullo!" Tanechka's voice reaches him. "Vanya! Vanetchka! Ivan Petrovitch, where are you? Hullo!"

"Hullo!" cries Osokin, jumping to his feet.

"Why did you go so far?" shouts Tanechka. "Come nearer!"

Osokin walks along the bank, scrambling through the bushes. He thinks she is still some way off, but suddenly the bushes part and he sees Tanechka in the middle of the stream with the water only up to her knees, standing quite naked, full of quite unexpected lines and curves, white and glistening with water, against the dark green background.

Seeing him, Tanechka laughs aloud, slips down into the water and, splashing with her hands, raises a shower of spray all round herself.

"Don't go so far away," she cries. "I'm afraid to stay alone in the wood."

For a moment she rises again from the water, provoking and defiant, and looks straight at Osokin. Their eyes meet, and at this moment it seems to him they know something that nobody else knows.

Osokin's breath fails him from joyous excitement. Tanechka laughs, puts out her tongue at him and plunges into deep water beneath the bushes.

"Why did you blush?" she cries, from the water, covering her breasts with her hands. "There! You've made me wet my hair. You're more afraid of me than I am of you. Go into the wood. I'm going to dress now. It's time to go home."

Osokin goes slowly up the hill listening to his beating heart, and sits down on the grass. It is all like a dream. Wild pigeons are cooing in the distance. A large spider drops slowly down from a fir tree, on a shining thread . . .

A few minutes later, Osokin gets up and walks down the other side of the knoll to meet Tanechka. She is dressed but still bare-footed. It seems to him that she blushes slightly when he comes up to her, but she looks at him just as provokingly and defiantly as when she was in the water.

"We must go home now," says Tanechka, as though nothing unusual had happened; but at the same time she again looks at Osokin in a slightly puzzled and, as it were, question - ing way.

Osokin wants to say something, but cannot find words. For several minutes they walk in silence. Tanechka nibbles a blade of grass, and glances at him occasionally.

Osokin, as he looks at her, cannot understand his emotions. Only yesterday, he could have struggled with her, trying to take a green beetle from her. Only that morning he could have taken her by the waist, so simply and easily, and held her to him. Now Tanechka has become different. He feels an enormous mystery in her, and this mystery frightens and troubles him, and puts a magic ring round her over which he cannot step.

Osokin wants to convey to Tanechka his desire to be sensible, but he feels that it would be silly to try. She might be offended. It would look as though she had been making up to him and he were refusing, though actually she has said nothing. And as for seeing her in the water—that was beautiful! Why should she be any more ashamed in front of him than that young birch.

"How meek you have become!" says Tanechka. "This morning you were quite different. What has happened to you? Have you a headache? Poor boy!" She passes her hand quickly over Osokin's head, pushes his cap over his eyes and, laughing, jumps away.

"And which do you prefer?" says Osokin, straightening his cap and feeling that his resolution to be sensible is sorely tried.

"As you are now, of course." Tanechka drawls the words. "Now, you are a regular Moscow young lady from boarding school; one can see that at once." And again she pushes his cap over his eyes and jumps away, laughing.

Osokin flings down the baskets of mushrooms, catches Tanechka, clasps her round her slim, supple waist, and presses his lips to her fresh, rosy cheek. Tanechka struggles away from him and laughs provokingly, and Osokin's kisses fall on her neck, her temples and her throat.

At last she twists herself out of his arms and cries:

"Look, you've upset the mushrooms. My mushrooms! Oh, you horrid thing!" She raises her hand as if threatening to strike Osokin. "Polkan, eat him up!"

Polkan jumps round them and barks.

Tanechka gathers up the mushrooms; Osokin gathers them up too: then seizing Tanechka by the hands he draws her to him and kisses her eyes, her lips, her cheeks. Tanechka does not resist. On the contrary, she lifts her face to him and, with a serious expression and downcast eyes, seems to listen to his kisses within herself.

Then they walk on down the green forest path, and from time to time Tanechka throws a glance at Osokin and laughs.

Next morning. At daybreak, Osokin slightly opens the door of his bedroom on the ground floor by the stairs, and looks into the long corridor. There is no one about. He opens the door, and Tanechka slips out. She is wearing a long yellow dressing gown and a shawl over her shoulders. In the doorway she turns, throws both arms round Osokin's neck, and kisses him on the lips with a long kiss that takes their breath away. Then, without a word, she wraps her head in the shawl and runs noiselessly upstairs.

Osokin watches her go, and when she has disappeared round the bend of the stair he goes back into his room.

He glances, with a vague smile, at the crumpled bed, goes to the window, flings it open, and leans out into the garden. He is at once enveloped in a wave of cool, moist, fragrant air, full of the rustle of green leaves, the voices of waking birds, the sunlight on the tree tops. He feels his chest expanding and he wants to draw in the whole garden in a breath.

He sits on the window sill, swings his legs outside and jumps down to the garden.

The grass is wet with shining drops of dew. The air is full of the scent of limes. Black Polkan suddenly appears, panting and wriggling with joy: he barks, and jumps up, putting his wet paws on Osokin's chest.

"Let's go to the lake, Polkan," says Osokin. "How could one go to bed now?"

Polkan wags his tail as though he understands, and rushes ahead down the avenue.

By the lake, some distance from the house, Osokin sits down on a high bank under some young fir trees. He puts his hand on Polkan's wet head which is laid on his knee, and, with a fleeting smile, sinks into thought. The sun struggles through the clouds and floods the whole lake with light.

"How strange it all is!" says Osokin. "And to think she came of her own accord. What an idiot Tolstoy is! What nonsense he wrote in 'The Kreutzer Sonata.' Where is the nastiness and coarseness in all this? Darling Tanechka! How I understand her now! Yes, this is the real thing, and the only real thing in the world. The truth is that it all belongs to woman, and only a woman has the right to decide. This must be understood, then everything else becomes quite different. But why do people not understand? Why have they created round it so much stupidity and vulgarity? And why do they hide from themselves the real meaning of it under all this mistrust and fear?"

He sits for a long time looking at the lake and stroking Polkan's head. What has just happened passes before him again and again, repeating itself in the same words, the same fluttering of the heart, and the same half-frightened and joyous sensations. A veil has suddenly fallen, and life has sparkled with a thousand lights, while the dark calumnies and lies which made love so frightening have rolled away like a cloud.

In the village beyond the hill a shepherd is playing his reed pipe, and the long trilling sounds spin out like golden threads, joyously and painfully touching his heart. Yes, yes, Tanechka! She came of her own accord. How beautiful it was! She came, and began to laugh and tease him, and he began to kiss her, and she laughed and said he was afraid of her. He could not have supposed that Tanechka was so experienced.

"But is she not right, and why may she not do as she likes? Of course she's right, of course she may! Why would it have been better if she had married a deacon in a country town, or the shopkeeper's son, Sinebriukhoff, which means Blue-belly? Instead of this, she found a sweetheart for herself without waiting for a wedding. Uncle certainly knows nothing, but even now Tanechka sometimes meets the young forest inspector from Zaozerye—And he is not her first sweetheart either. But who could blame her? She is so wonderful. How sweet and natural everything is about her! How softly she laughed when she let me undress her and kiss her. What warm lips she has, and what a sensitive body . . . her breasts, shoulders, legs. It's extraordinary and marvellous! How can people slander love in the way they do, and make of it a vice and a crime? All those disgusting words, those vile expressions . . . all the medical, the physiological terms . . . as if there were anything like that in it. It is like a chemical analysis of a violin. No, it isn't! It's exactly like the sound of that pipe—there are no words for it."

The sound of the reed pipe draws slowly nearer, and in Osokin's soul many forgotten thoughts are stirred, troubling, but very familiar; something comes back to memory, something rises to the surface from the dark depths.

Now before him Osokin sees the lake all afire in the sun, and the white clouds fringed with gold, and the softly rustling green reeds.

"How incredibly beautiful it all is," he says. "But why does death exist? Or perhaps there is no death? For a moment I can understand that. Nothing dies. Everything exists forever. It is we who go away from it, lose sight of it. Yesterday exists. Tanechka in the water and I afraid to look at her. This has not died and it cannot die. I can always go back to it. But there is a mystery about it; this mystery we call death. Yet in truth death is simply our failure to understand something. I feel this now. Why can it not always be felt? Then we should fear nothing . . . and it is Tanechka who has given

me this. At last I understand that this is not merely the best
but also the most important, the most essential thing in life.
When *it* comes, everything else must be silent and give way to
it. How can one be 'sensible' in relation to it? Those two hours
are worth more than anything in the world. If I knew that
my head was to be cut off for it to-day, I should kiss Tanechka just the same ... And now, I want to fly over the lake
as I fly in my dreams!"

CHAPTER XX
UNCLE

A FEW DAYS LATER. Tanechka is sitting on the veranda with some needlework. Osokin comes in from the garden.

"I'm going to the Zuevo swamp after dinner. Would anyone like to come with me?" says Tanechka in a sing-song voice, smiling slyly without raising her head.

"I should, Tanechka dear," says Osokin, coming up to her. "But, you know, we ought to be a little more careful. For the last few days we have been together all the time, and it's too noticeable."

"Well, what of it?" says Tanechka, biting off her thread and glancing up at him.

"Well, I think it may all end very badly. It seems to me that Uncle is watching us very suspiciously, and the servants are probably talking already."

"Little coward!" says Tanechka, scornfully. "A regular young lady, afraid of everything. Well, let them see, let them talk, I'm not afraid of anything." She tosses her head defiantly.

"Tanechka darling, don't be angry," says Osokin, "Just now you look exactly like White Legs when she is naughty."

"You're always laughing at me," says Tanechka, pouting, "either I look like White Legs or God knows what . . ."

"Don't be angry, darling."

"Are you coming for mushrooms?"

"Kiss me, and I'll come."

"Oh, you ask too much!"

"Well, let me kiss your neck."

"One little finger . . . Oh, bother! I quite forgot, they are laying the table. I must see to the *zakouska*."

Tanechka runs away.

"She's a darling," says Osokin to himself, "but we're walking on very thin ice, and it's sure to break. How suddenly it has all come about!"

He follows Tanechka.

In the dining-room Tanechka is bending over the table stirring a mustard dressing for the herring. Osokin steals up to her and kisses her on the neck. She screams, and strikes him with a napkin. Osokin clasps her round the waist, holds her whole body to him, and kisses her on the mouth. Tanechka resists feebly, then turns in Osokin's arms offering him one after the other her cheek, her ear, her neck, to be kissed.

At that moment, the door opens and Osokin's uncle appears and stops on the threshold. Tanechka jumps away from Osokin.

"There now," thinks Osokin, "I knew this would happen." He feels vexed and ashamed, and his heart is thumping violently.

He is annoyed at not being able to hide his confusion, but at the same time he is amazed—so completely has everything happened as he had anticipated.

His uncle looks at them and, without speaking, walks to the table. Osokin feels very foolish. The worst of it is having to sit at table and pretend that nothing has happened. Tanechka, confused and blushing, serves the soup, trying not to look at either Osokin or his uncle. The uncle is obviously furious, but says nothing. Osokin's one desire is to get away.

His uncle reluctantly swallows a glass of vodka, and, without touching the *zakouska*, takes his soup.

The silence becomes oppressive.

"Where did you go?" his uncle asks Osokin, in an unfriendly voice.

"To Orehovo for the letters and newspapers," answers Osokin.

"A groom could have been sent."

"What does he wish to imply by that?" thinks Osokin.

"That I'm doing nothing, probably."

"You just gad about," says his uncle as though he were answering him. Then, after a long pause, he adds:

"I want to speak to you. Come to my room at four."

At last dinner is over.

Osokin goes into the garden, then walks round the house. Tanechka is nowhere to be seen.

Osokin has an unpleasant feeling—a kind of disgust at all that has happened, but at the same time, he notices with astonishment that he is very calm at heart, much calmer than he was in the morning. It is as if something has happened that was bound to happen, and now he feels easier, because nothing depends on him. "What will be, will be!" He does not want to think.

"It's all the same," he says to himself. "The devil take it! I knew it would happen, but I could do nothing differently. If everything were to be repeated, I should do the same thing again. No doubt it was silly to kiss Tanechka in the dining-room, but sooner or later we should probably have been caught. I wonder what the old man is going to say. But, whatever happens, I know I could not have given up Tanechka."

Osokin walks to the copse at the end of the garden, passes through it and comes out into a field. He sits down at the edge of the wood and remains there, almost without thought, for a long time. Then he comes home. It is still only three o'clock.

"Where is the young mistress?" he asks a maid who is running across the courtyard.

"The lady from Polivanovo just called: the young mistress went away with her on our horses. They left their horses here to rest."

Polivanovo is about thirty miles away.

"Why the devil did Tanechka go there?" thinks Osokin. "That means she will not be home till to-morrow night. Most likely my uncle sent her off. What can he have in his mind?"

Osokin feels bored and depressed. He walks back to the garden and sits under an old apple tree, smoking.

At four o'clock he goes to his uncle's room. His uncle is sitting in a leather armchair in front of a big desk. On the desk lies a sealed letter.

"Sit down," says his uncle without looking at him. He evidently dislikes having to speak to Osokin and wants to get it over as quickly as possible.

In his uncle's mood, and in what he is going to say to him, Osokin feels something of that dull, serious world of grown-up people which is always so hostile to him and so utterly unlike the fantastic world of kisses, daydreams, Tanechka's bare shoulders, sunrise over the lake and solitary rides along forest paths. He is acutely aware of the profound inner hostility between these two worlds.

"Your mother wrote to me not long before her death," says his uncle, "and I promised to look after you."

Osokin looks at the silver inkstand on the desk. If a little arched bridge could be made between the two ink pots, it would look like a pond at Sokolniki. What is his uncle saying?

"I see now that you are only idling here, and doing nothing. I have decided to send you to Petersburg. It is no use thinking about foreign universities; since you have been expelled from school, it means you are no good for that. Don't interrupt me! What I am saying is this: I see how you are working. Nothing will come of it. So I have decided to send you to military school. If you work, you will become an officer. You will go to Petersburg. Here is a letter to Colonel Yermiloff. He prepares boys for the examination for military schools. You will live in his house. Here is money for the journey. Yermiloff will provide you with funds for clothes and other expenses. Pack your things. The train leaves Gorelovo at eight-thirty. If you leave here at seven, you will be just in time."

His uncle gets up.

"I am going to town," he says. Then still without looking at Osokin, he holds out his hand and, after a hurried handshake, walks out.

Osokin goes to his room. He is hurt and upset and there is a lump in his throat. At the same time he feels with astonishment that he is *almost glad*. About what? He cannot answer himself. But something new and unknown lies ahead. Something will happen to-morrow that did not happen yesterday. This *new* something already attracts him. He has never been to Petersburg and has always dreamed about it. But what of Tanechka? That saddens him and there is a pain at his heart. At the same time there rises in him a more and more unpleasant feeling towards his uncle. He is now ashamed to admit to himself that he had almost begun to grow fond of the old man.

"If he can treat me like this," thinks Osokin, "then I'm glad it happened in this way. If he had wanted to, he could have found a thousand other solutions. Why does he think that he has the right to dispose of us? Of course I shan't let him see anything now. But if he imagines that he can make me give up Tanechka, he's greatly mistaken."

Many different plans at once begin to form in Osokin's mind. He is not going to prepare for any military school in Petersburg. He will find some journalistic work, or translations from English and Italian. He will prepare for the University and send for Tanechka to come to him.

But he must write to Tanechka about this now so that she will wait for him. He must not let her think that he will forget her as her other sweethearts have done.

He takes a sheet of paper and writes:

Darling Tanechka:

Uncle is sending me to Petersburg to prepare for a military school, but I am going to work for the University examination. Don't forget me. We shall meet soon. I won't tell you yet how and when, but wait for a letter from me. I'll send it to Gorelovo to be called for. When the letter arrives, they'll let you know from there. I kiss you many times as I did by the lake, do you remember? Your, I. O.

He seals the letter and looks at his watch. It is after five o'clock. He is aware of a strange feeling: little more than an hour has passed since the talk with his uncle, but it seems to Osokin that he himself is no longer here. Everything has become remote. The strongest feeling in him is one of impatience and a desire to get away as quickly as possible.

"I shall give the letter to Mishka," thinks Osokin, "and tell him to give it to Tanechka in the garden, not in the house. He will manage it all right.

"Good," he says to himself, "now we shall see. But I must pack. Yes, I understand why it is almost pleasant to know that I am leaving here. All the time I had the irritating feeling of being watched—because I don't work, because I go riding too often, and then Tanechka . . . In any case, I couldn't have lived here for long. I wish to have the right to do what I want, and not what someone else thinks good or necessary for me. I have never submitted to anything, and I never shall."

Two hours later. Osokin, with his trunk, is being driven to the station in a troika with bells. White Legs canters on the right side of the middle horse. Osokin's heart is heavy, and hopeless thoughts creep into his mind. He thinks about his mother again and how, when she was alive, he did none of the things that he wanted to do for her.

"All this was important then," he says to himself, "but now nothing seems to matter. I don't want anything and I don't care about anything."

For some reason there arises in his mind the memory of the magician's room and their last conversation; all comes back to him. It feels very real, but at the same time more like a dream—a very strange dream which is more real than reality and compared with which all reality becomes like a dream.

With a clatter of hoofs the troika crosses the bridge at

a slow trot. White Legs shies at the river and, dancing a little, presses nearer to the middle horse. The bells jingle more slowly. Osokin's heart throbs with a strange pain. Yesterday morning he walked here with Tanechka ... And besides, a long, long time ago it had been the same; there was the same troika, the same river, the same piercing anguish in his heart. It has all been before. Osokin feels unutterably sad and wants to cry.

At the same time, in the mysterious to-morrow, something flickers, something beckons, something inevitable and alluring is felt.

CHAPTER XXI
THE DEVIL'S MECHANICS

THREE AND A HALF YEARS LATER. Osokin is a second year 'junker' in a Moscow Military School. He is about twenty. In another six months his course will be finished and he will be promoted to officer.

Sunday evening. Osokin, looking very well drilled with straight broad shoulders in his black Military School tunic and red shoulder straps with gold edges, black leather belt, wide breeches and shining top boots, is at a party in the flat of his old school friend, Leontieff, who is now a student at a technical high school. The guests, several young men, a dragoon officer, an old actor, two French girls and two music hall actresses, are playing *chemin de fer*.

Osokin is sitting by the *zakouska* table with a glass of wine, smoking a cigarette and watching the players. The two French girls and one of the actresses are very pretty, over-dressed, over-scented and heavily powdered. They are laughing and shouting. There is nothing jarring or unpleasant about them, but at the same time they belong to a definite type. His attention is more attracted by the fourth, a strangely thoughtful-looking, fair girl in a black dress cut square at the neck. She does not catch the eye at once, but is really the most interesting of them all. She has a fine profile and long dark eyelashes, and her manner is remarkably calm, simple and dignified. People do not talk to her in the same way as they do to the others. She gives the impression of being well-bred; wherever she might be, she would know what to say and how to say it.

At the same time one feels that in her, more than in all the other three put together, there is something that goes to the head like champagne. One feels that she can be different if she chooses. Osokin looks at her arms, bare to the elbow, white with small blue veins, and is most strongly and vividly aware of the woman in her.

This is the third time they have met, and it seems to him that during their short and insignificant conversations *another* conversation has been going on between them. It is pleasant to talk to her; she knows everything, and is interested in everything.

She feels his glance and turns towards him. "Come and help me," she says, "I am losing all the time."

Osokin goes to the table.

"I'll have to go soon," he says, "it's not worth while beginning."

"Just try! Play for me."

There is a faint, hardly perceptible scent about her that is like herself, and, as Osokin bends over her cards, he sees the curve of her breasts in the opening of her dress. He feels gay and happy. He sits down beside her and moves his chair quite close to hers. She smiles; and Osokin is seized by that peculiar feeling he knows so well—*everything will now happen just as he wants, but afterwards, he will have to pay dearly for it.*

"Well, so be it!" says Osokin in his mind, aware of the warmth that comes from the girl.

The cards are dealt.

Osokin picks up her cards. Several people draw cards. Osokin has seven.

"One little card," he says.

He is given a card. It is a two!

"Eight!" says one of the players.

"Nine!" says Osokin, and moves a fair-sized heap of gold and silver towards his neighbor.

"Bravo, bravo!" she cries. "No, you mustn't go. I won't let you. Nothing on earth would have induced me to draw to a seven."

"Sometimes it has to be done," says Osokin, "but only sometimes."

"And how is one to know?"

"One must feel when it is necessary and when it is not."

"Well, please 'feel' for me to-night."

"Alas! I can only go on feeling for half an hour," he says. "I have leave until midnight, so I must be back at the School at five minutes to twelve."

"And if you are late, will they put you in the corner?"

"Worse! I shall lose a mark and then I'll not get into the first category, and that means I shall not be able to choose a good regiment. They are keeping an eye on me as it is, and if I'm late again I may be expelled."

"Could they possibly expel you for that?"

"With the greatest of ease. You see, they are trying to teach us discipline, so special importance is attached to everything. Leave is till midnight, and that means I may die, but I must be back at School before midnight! But that's nothing; there are worse things. For instance, we have no right to answer, no matter what we are told. This is the most difficult. Imagine being told something very unjust, something that never happened, being accused of something of which you know nothing. And you must be silent."

"I should never be able to do that," declares Osokin's neighbor with emphasis.

"Then you would be expelled from a military school."

The game begins again. Osokin wins. Champagne cup is brought in. Leontieff comes over to Osokin and his partner.

"Well, Vanya, have you lost?" he says.

"No damn it! On the contrary, I'm afraid I'm going to win. I have already foretold it to myself."

"Can you foretell the future?" asks the lady.

"Yes. I know everything beforehand," says Osokin, "only not for everybody."

"Can you foretell something for me?"

"For you, I don't know, probably not. But I frequently

foretell things for myself, and sometimes it is distinctly unpleasant. You understand, I often know beforehand what must happen to me, but I can change nothing. It's as though I were under a spell."

"Well, what do you know now?"

Osokin laughs. "I know that I shall be thrown out of the School if I don't go back at once. Really, I must go."

"Oh, what a pity! I shall lose everything again without you. Can't you manage to stay somehow?"

"Well, I can," says Osokin, "but it will be very complicated. I shall have to be ill and it will be necessary to get a doctor's certificate."

The game goes on, and Osokin wins again.

"I know I ought not to be doing this," he says. "It's only for you. Well, if I lose, I'll go. Right?"

Osokin wins. The game continues.

"Well, it looks as though I were ill already," says Osokin with a sigh, passing the money to his neighbor and gently pressing the tips of her fingers, "and I know what will come of it. You cannot imagine how tired I am, sometimes, of knowing everything beforehand."

"How can you be so sure?"

"Oh, I know for certain that something very unpleasant is going to happen," says Osokin, "but I don't care. Sometimes I get into such a mood that I want to act against all reason and contrary to everything—let come what may!"

"And you know only that something unpleasant is going to happen, nothing more?" says the lady, looking sideways at Osokin and smiling with her eyes.

Osokin suddenly understands that something has already been decided between them and he feels aghast that he could have been such a fool as even to have thought of going back to the School. Of course he will see her home . . . The game continues. He wins more than anyone at the table and flirts with his partner.

The guests leave in the early hours of the morning, and

Osokin goes off with his lady.

"I'll come back to you," he says to Leontieff, taking him aside.

"You should say, 'If I am allowed to.' This isn't a military school, my friend! It's no use your trying to break discipline here!"

Three weeks later. Osokin, grown very thin, is at Leontieff's flat. He has been expelled from the Military School and sent to the regiment to finish the time of his service as a conscript.

"Now, Vanya, tell me how it all happened," says Leontieff.

"Well, first, I went away with . . . you know?"

"Yes, Anna Stepanovna."

"Well, I stayed with her. She is wonderful, but that's not the point. I had to leave in the daytime. It was inconvenient for her to keep me there till evening. Well, I walked out of the house and at the very first corner I ran into a gendarme colonel. Naturally, he immediately took my pass and sent me to the School to report myself to the officer on duty. I was put straight under arrest. Other old sins were remembered against me, and they kept me locked up for three weeks. That in itself is no treat, I can assure you. So, to conclude, I'm expelled and reduced to the ranks, and have to go to an infantry regiment at the back of beyond, to Central Asia on the Persian frontier. Thank God, I've been given three days' leave and allowed to go at my own expense."

"That's nice business! You're as lucky as a drowned man."

"Exactly, though I never understand why a drowned man is considered so lucky."

"Anna Stepanovna kept asking about you. She had to go away, but she didn't want to go until she heard about you. We tried, through Krutitsky, to find out for her whether you were alive or dead. We were told that you were alive but locked up."

"Has she gone to Petersburg?"

"Yes. What are you going to do now?"

"What can I do? Only one thing—join the regiment. After that, we shall see. But think how damnable it is that I knew it all beforehand."

"If you knew, why did you do it?"

"Yes! You try not to do it! You funny fellow! Evidently you have no idea what kind of devil's mechanics this is. The whole trick is, that nothing is done all at once; everything is done little by little. This is what I'm only just beginning to understand. And one can do—God knows what, little by little! You never even notice it yourself until everything turns out as it had to turn out. From a distance you can see everything, but when you come close to things you no longer see the whole, you see only separate parts, little details that mean nothing. No, my dear man, it's such a trap that the devil himself would break his leg in it. So, once more, I am left with nothing. But do you realize that I'm not in the least sorry? I don't think any of you can understand that."

"Well, then, we must give you a good send-off."

"Yes, nothing else remains; you may, if you like."

"But, after all, what are you going to do?"

"What can I do? I shall be a soldier, nothing more. They may let me go soon, and when I am free I shall see. I don't think my uncle will want to know me any more. I shan't even write to him. So what can I say now? It seems to me that some change must come, but where it will come from, I don't know."

CHAPTER XXII
PARIS

FOUR YEARS LATER. Osokin is a student in Paris. Just as he
was finishing his military service his aunt died, leaving him
a small legacy which enabled him to go abroad. At first he
moved from place to place, went to Switzerland, stayed for a
year in England, then came to Paris, and for the last two
years, he has been living there. He is attending lectures by
various professors, but still cannot make a choice of any
particular faculty.

Beautiful pale sunny autumn day with a slight mist over
the river.

Osokin and an English girl-student, Valerie Dale, are walking along the Seine embankment by the bookstalls. She is a
tall blonde girl with hair the color of autumn leaves, a fine
profile and pensive dark grey eyes. She belongs to a rich
English family and dresses beautifully, so that even in Paris
people always turn and look at her.

"But really she is an awfully clever girl," says Osokin to
himself.

She is the best pupil of old Sorel. She studies mediaeval
history and art and has written a very interesting mono-
graph—'Builders of Cathedrals.'

"Where does she get these ideas?" thinks Osokin. Sorel
never had any like that. And how extraordinary that she
knows Russian and Russian literature and history.

One day they had a long talk about Pushkin and about
Russian masons. She told him then that she had begun with

Russian and intended to go to Russia, but later became quite absorbed by Gothic art and its period.

Osokin looks at Valerie. She is wearing what is evidently a very expensive coat with fine sables, and a wide-brimmed hat with an ostrich feather. Osokin always admires her feet in trim Paris shoes with high heels.

They continue a conversation which started when they were in the Louvre.

"I believe in destiny," says Osokin. "I know that our future is written down somewhere and that we merely read it page by page. Besides that, I had strange fantasies as a boy. It seemed to me that I had lived before; for instance, I knew Paris—though of course I had never been here. Even now there are times when I feel that I have lived in Paris before. When I met with Nietzsche's ideas on eternal recurrence, I recalled all these fantasies. And now I am sure that everything really does repeat itself."

"Do you know Stevenson's—Robert Louis Stevenson's—'Song of the Morrow'?" asks his companion.

Osokin starts, and looks at her.

"Why what's the matter?" she asks.

"How astonishing! How could I have forgotten it? Of course I know it. How does it begin?"

"*The King of Duntrine had a daughter when he was old,*" begins the girl slowly, "*and she was the fairest King's daughter between two seas . . .*"

Osokin listens to these words like one bewitched. Scenes in which he can scarcely believe pass in succession through his mind: the morning at school when he repeated the beginning of this tale to himself in order to prove that he had lived before; all the elusive thoughts and incomprehensible sensations connected with the magician, and with what—to him, at school—appeared to be the past, and which now—here in Paris—appears to be the fantastic and impossible future. What does it all mean? And once more this tale . . . It seems to Osokin that if only he could stop his thoughts for a moment he would understand everything—but his thoughts rush past so quickly that he can catch nothing. All that remains with him is the general impression that everything is turning upside down: the past becoming the future and the future the past. For a moment he feels that if only he were able, or if only he dared, to think of the future as of something that had been before, he would see it as clearly as he can see yesterday.

At the same time there comes over him the old familiar sensation—which used to come so often but now comes more and more rarely—that everything around him has been before. In the same way the river flowed by, the same mist hung over the water; the same greenish Paris sky smiled faintly from above and the last leaves flew from the trees. In the same way the girl's golden curls escaped from her black hat, and in the same way her voice sounded . . .

"Do you remember the end, the very end?" asks Osokin.

"Yes, I remember," and slowly she recites the end of the tale:

"And the King's daughter of Duntrine got her to that part of the beach where strange things had been done in the ancient ages; and there she sat her down. The sea foam ran to her feet, and the dead leaves swarmed about her back, and the veil blew about her face in the blowing of the wind. And when she lifted up her eyes, there was the daughter of a King come walking on the beach. Her hair was like the spun gold, and her eyes like pools in a river, and she had no thought for the morrow and no power upon the hour, after the manner of simple men."

"It's amazing," says Osokin to himself. "Why do these words arouse so many memories in me? I feel that the memories come directly from words, apart from their meaning, as if I know something connected with them but every year forget it more and more."

"It is remarkable, that tale," he says aloud. "How do you understand 'the man in the hood'? Who is he or what is he?"

"I don't know," the girl answers slowly, "and I feel that it's not necessary even to try to understand; such things must simply be felt. I feel it as I do music, and interpretations of music have always seemed ridiculous to me."

They reach the Place St. Michel and she takes a *fiacre*. Osokin says good-bye to her.

"Will you be at my brother's this evening?" she asks.

"Probably, but I don't know yet."

"Tell him that I'm expecting him to-morrow."

Osokin walks across the bridge towards the Cité.

"Shall I go there or not?" he asks, when he is alone. "Seriously speaking, I should not go. Bob himself and his friends are too absurdly rich. Valerie and he are quite easy-going and mix with all sorts of people here, but they belong to a rather important family in England. Valerie is an interesting girl, it's true, and however it may be in view of our different positions in life, I know that if I let things develop they may bring us to quite unexpected results. Even now I feel that there is something unusual in our friendship as though some very brilliant and fiery sparks fly between us from time to time."

"And yet I know that we should never get on well together. First there are those millions, and then I think that Valerie is too virtuous for me. She will always be even-tempered, charming and reasonable. I am sure I should soon run away from a woman like that, and then she would suffer. She is the type of one of Turgeneff's heroines. She is decidedly too good for me. But if Loulou finds out about her she will scratch my eyes out.

"Loulou is absurdity incarnate, but the most enchanting absurdity possible. One never knows what to expect from her. Each day she is different. I am constantly parting from one Loulou and meeting a different one. Yesterday she made a scene because I was not aware of her when she was walking behind me in the street. She saw me in the distance, caught up with me, walked behind me—and I never felt it! That means I don't love her! 'I may go to my Russia and she will go to her Marseilles,' and so on and so on. And last week— O God!—she dreamed that I threw her little Pekinese dog out of the window, and for three days she wouldn't let me into her room. She shouted that I was a barbarian, that she would never forgive me for it, and that she was afraid of me—and God knows what else! Sometimes I want to whip her for all these absurdities, but she is a real woman. Yes, I'll buy her that brooch with the yellow stones, and for that especially, I'll go and play roulette with the millionaires' sons to-day—though to tell the truth I ought not to. There's too strong a smell of millions there, and it's not good for me. Well, let's decide: this must be for the last time. I would probably not go, only I'm so awfully bored. Loulou is a darling, but I spent all day and all the evening with her yesterday, and it's better that we should not see each other every day. In large doses we begin to get on each other's nerves. Besides, Loulou is much too primitive to spend whole days with. But what else can I do with myself? Stay at home and read, or sit at a café, or go and listen to the 'comrades'—no, this is too stupid . . . But it's a curious thing, I begin to feel that life here is running too smoothly; it's too easy-going, almost bourgeois in fact, a regular 'slippers and dressing-gown' existence—not my style at all, and it bores me."

A few hours later. Osokin is at Bob Dale's expensive flat. A roulette wheel is on the table. In the room there are several American and English students and painters, and a young Russian prince who has just come into a legacy. They are smoking and drinking whisky and soda and champagne, and they all crowd round the roulette table. Stakes are high. The prince has lost more than a hundred thousand francs, and the whole table is littered with gold and bank notes. Osokin puts twenty francs at a time on the numbers, and loses. After losing his last gold piece, he leaves the table. The prince wins a large stake and the bank passes to him.

Osokin gulps down two glasses of whisky and soda. He is angry with himself.

"The devil take them!" he thinks. "They can fling away tens of thousands, but for me, five hundred francs is a lot of money. All the same, it was stupid to bring so little. In the course of the evening the luck is bound to turn, and I could have had dozens of chances to win back my money."

"Why do you sit there alone?" says Bob, coming up to him. "Try this champagne; it's King Edwards' favorite brand. I'm beginning to like it myself."

"I've been losing," says Osokin. "Can I stake checks for one hundred francs each?"

"But why bother to write out so many checks? I'll cash any sum you like," says a tall young American with a good-humored, clean-shaven face, and smooth, pale yellow hair. He is preparing absinthe for himself by slowly dropping water into it through sugar. "How much would you like?"

He pulls a handful of gold and bank notes out of his trouser pocket and counts it.

"I have English money," he says, "two, three, five hundred pounds. Will that do?"

"It's far too much," laughs Osokin. "Give me a hundred. That will be two thousand, five hundred francs."

He writes out a check and gives it to the American.

The American shoves the money and the check into his pocket, takes a sip from his mixture and, glass in hand, strolls over to the roulette table. Osokin also gets up and follows him.

A quarter of an hour later, Osokin has nothing left. He has lost not only the hundred pounds, but all the hundred-franc checks he had written out before.

"I told you it wouldn't be enough. Would you like some more?" says the yellow-haired American good-naturedly, sitting down beside him. "Let's try this champagne."

"Give me another thousand francs," says Osokin, "I must win back what I've lost."

He writes out another check.

Deep down in himself he feels that he is being a fool. He has already lost so much that he is afraid to admit it to himself. To go on playing is madness. He knows that he ought to get up and go, but instead, he drinks two glasses of champagne and returns to the roulette table.

He puts a hundred francs on red, and wins. He puts another hundred on black, and wins again. This encourages him.

"I must try the numbers again," he says to himself. "If I win back what I've lost, I'll put the money into my left-hand pocket and not touch it any more. I'll only play with what I win."

He stakes a hundred francs a time on the numbers and loses each time. Ten minutes later he again has no money.

"I must go," he says to himself. He wants to get out into the fresh air. He is already tired of the game. The champagne, the whisky and the smoke of the pipes and cigars have made him feel dizzy, but he is annoyed at having lost so much and feels that he cannot and will not go.

Once more he writes out a check, cashes it, and sits down to play. At one moment, he wins, then he loses and is short of money again. Then he wins again. Then things get worse and he increases his stakes. At last, after losing steadily for some time, he leaves the table.

"I must see how I stand," he says to himself. "I believe I've gone too far."

He takes out his check book and adds up the total amount of the checks he has signed. And as he counts, he grows cold and frightened—although he knows all the time how it will be.

"There!" he says to himself. "Is it really true?" and he knows now that he had a presentiment that it would be exactly like this.

His check book shows that he has only three hundred francs left. He has lost more than thirty thousand francs—all that remained from his legacy. He makes out a check for three hundred francs and goes to the table.

"Twenty-five," he says.

The ball is running.

"Twenty-six," says the prince, who holds the bank. "Who staked on twenty-six?"

Osokin walks away from the table. Everyone is occupied with the game. No one notices him. He finds his hat and goes away.

Osokin walks down the stairs and out into the street. Something monstrously absurd has happened, changing his whole life again at one stroke. He does not want to believe it. At the same time he knows it is the truth, the disgusting, hideous truth which he has encountered many times in his life before. It is not yet felt—everything is still the same, the street, the houses—but it will make itself felt to-morrow. With the instinct of a man who has been through all kinds of troubles and surprises, Osokin knows that it is better to look this truth straight in the face without trying to deceive himself or put off recognizing it.

"I knew it would be so," he says to himself. "But now that it has happened there must be no weakness, no regret, no repentance. That's the chief thing, otherwise one might go mad. I used to be able to survive all kinds of catastrophes; let's see how I'll survive this one. *I did it myself. I myself* am guilty, and I *myself* must get over it. No one will even know about it. At Bob's they probably never noticed that I lost so much. What are thirty thousand francs to them, when there was nearly a half a million on the table? Well, this is a fine brooch for Loulou! Now, I must think. The point is that I have lost everything I had to live on until my studies were over. Obviously, I must go away. To change my style of living here and live on what I might earn would be impossible. And what could I earn? No, I shall go either to America or to Russia. Poor Loulou! She will never understand what has happened, and she won't believe me if I tell her that I've lost thirty thousand francs. She will simply think that I want to get rid of her. It would hurt too much, and I have no right to do that. I'll have to invent some lie to tell her, and the sooner I go away the better."

Osokin reaches home and spends the whole night sorting out his things; tearing up letters, packing, and writing notes.

By morning, everything is ready. Dead tired, he lies down on the sofa without undressing and falls asleep.

About three hours later he wakes, and at once sits up on the sofa. He remembers everything; he remembers also that he must keep a hold on himself and not admit that awful moment of awakening after an unexpected disaster when a weak man asks himself: But perhaps it's not true, perhaps it never happened?

"Yes," he says to himself, as though continuing the conversation with himself he began the night before, "I must go away to-day. I'll shoot myself if I stay till to-morrow. Poor Loulou! But she will get that brooch with the yellow stones after all. How lucky I had these two thousand francs at home! Now, it seems quite a fortune. I'll go to Moscow, then I shall see . . . How strange it is that I feel it so little! Last night I was afraid to go to bed; I thought I should go mad when I wakened and remembered everything. But now I have the feeling that it all had to be. There's one thing though—I must get away from here as soon as possible. To delay would be too painful. If I have to go, I have to! Evidently this is fate. And I know now that I had a premonition about it, and even knew it beforehand. This means I shall not see Valerie any more. How strange! I'm almost sorry now. It seems to me that we should have come to something. It was always so pleasant to meet her, and we had so much to tell each other. I laughed at her, but actually she interested me much more than I realized—and perhaps I was quite unjust to her. She always appeared to be too cold, but that may be because she doesn't know herself and only needs waking up.

"Well, no matter, all that is already ancient history. Valerie, Loulou, the whole of Paris, have become almost unreal. I feel as though I had dreamed it and now that I am awake, it doesn't exist any more. But other dreams are appearing instead. I see the magician again, and remember how we talked. And now this seems quite real, more real than what happened yesterday,—well, enough of philosophy! I must decide what to do. First, have I the courage to go and see Loulou, or shall I write to her? No, I ought to go. I'll say this: 'I have received a telegram. My uncle is dying, I must go at once' . . . Yes, when I think of Loulou I begin to feel very unhappy. I wish I were already on the train. When shall I stop performing such operations on myself? I don't believe there is anyone who has turned his life upside down in the way I've always done. But how strange! Again I have the sensation that all this has happened before. And when I think of Moscow, I feel as if something new and unknown begins to draw me there. Yesterday, when I parted from Valerie, for some reason I asked myself what I should say if I were seeing her for the last time. Evidently, deep down in myself, I was aware that I should again destroy everything . . . And I didn't even *want* to go to Bob's, but at the same time I wanted to try my luck. Everything had been going so smoothly during the last few years that I began to get bored. Well, I've tried it. Now I must start everything from the beginning again; and I don't even know where to begin. Well, I'll begin with a ticket to Moscow and the brooch to Loulou!"

He gets up from the sofa and looks round. Then he puts on his coat and goes out.

CHAPTER XXIII
ZINAIDA

EIGHTEEN MONTHS LATER. Osokin is living in Moscow. At
first he hoped to earn some money and return to Paris, but
things have not gone successfully, and finally he has begun
to live from day to day, at times expecting that some change
will come of itself, and at times ceasing to expect anything at
all. He has tried giving French lessons; later he found some
translations to do; then he remembered that he was considered a very promising pupil in a famous fencing school in
Paris and began to give fencing lessons.

He also writes poetry—but does not wish to publish it.
Most of all, he dreams of going somewhere very far away, to
Australia or New Zealand, to begin life afresh.

One day, in the street, he meets his Military School friend,
Krutitsky, who invites him to the country house where he
lives during the summer. Krutitsky is now an officer studying
for the Military Academy. He has made a very successful
marriage. At his house, Osokin is introduced to his sister who
has just returned from Italy where she has been living for
seven years.

Before he goes to Krutitsky's, Osokin knows that he will see
Zinaida Krutitsky there, and for some reason he expects a
great deal from this meeting. He heard so much about her
while he was at the Military School, and he knows her well
from photographs.

But actually everything happens in a most ordinary way.
They talk of trivial things, and Osokin gets no particular impression. Zinaida seems to him to be a society girl, evidently

destined to make a good marriage, much occupied with herself, and living with artificial interests which he does not understand—amateur theatricals for charity or a private concert given by some musical celebrity. Even her face does not attract him very much; it seems inexpressive and bored.

"How strange!" Osokin says to himself on his way home. "When I was at the Military School, I was unusually excited by anything I heard about Krutitsky's sister. It seemed to me that I had known her in the past. I was almost in love with her from her photographs and from the things I heard about her. This was connected with my fantasies about the magician and my former life. I liked to dream about how I should meet Zinaida; and now that I have met her, I feel that we can have nothing in common. She would understand nothing of my life. They are such comfortable people, particularly Krutitsky and his wife . . . And really it is absurd that I should have expected anything different from this meeting. We live in worlds so remote one from the other. No, I must decide definitely. I'll work and save money for six months, then I'll go away. There is absolutely nothing for me to do here."

A week later. Osokin, finding it dull alone in town, goes to see Krutitsky again. No one is at home except Zinaida. Krutitsky and his wife have gone to their other place in the country to see relatives and are not coming back till the next day.

For some reason this pleases Osokin very much. Zinaida is on the veranda, with a French novel, and she too is evidently pleased to see him. But the conversation drags, and there is a feeling of strain. Osokin is annoyed at not being able to touch the right note with Zinaida; each subject they begin somehow breaks off by itself at the third sentence.

"Let's go for a walk," says Zinaida, after one of the long pauses. "This house and garden make me sleepy."

To-day, Zinaida appears quite different to Osokin, but he still cannot make her out. She is very much of a woman. At the same time one feels something distant in her. She looks older than she probably is. She has a pale face which, at a first glance, appears to be not sufficiently clearly drawn. But when one looks longer, the fine, clearcut features show themselves as through a veil. She has lazy movements; something in her reminds one of an Oriental woman. 'Tartar family.' Most wonderful of all are her eyes. They are not very large, but dark, sometimes like velvet, sometimes limpid; their expression is constantly changing, sometimes sparkling with a dozen fires, now almost slumbering. Osokin begins to think that those eyes must have many other expressions, and already his curiosity is aroused.

They walk side by side through a small pine wood. Osokin observes everything about Zinaida.

She is dressed in a rather unusual style of her own—a loose dress of pale Chinese silk with much lace, and bronze shoes with pearl buttons. She has brought a sunshade and she covers her head from the sun with a yellow scarf. She uses no scent.

Her profile, her eyes, and especially her mouth attract Osokin's glance more and more.

They come to the river and the boats. Osokin helps Zinaida into one, and then rows up the river in the shadow of the trees.

"Do you know," says Osokin almost without expecting it himself, "I was in love with you when I was at the Military School, but I imagined you to be quite different."

"This becomes interesting," she says, laughing. "How did you imagine me then?"

"I don't know—it is difficult to say exactly—but in some way, different. It seemed to me, too, that I had known you earlier, long before I saw your photograph at your brother's. It was connected with some very complicated dreams and fantasies I had about my former life; about a magician of whom I believe I dreamed—and who foretold my future. In some way you were connected with it. I mean that when I saw your photograph I was convinced it was of you that the magician had spoken."

"But what did he say exactly?"

"Would you believe it, I've forgotten! I remember 'all that will be has been.' "

Zinaida asks, "Why do magicians say such incomprehensible things? And what kind of magician was he? You say you saw him in a dream?"

"Perhaps it was a dream, perhaps it was real, perhaps I invented him. I don't know," says Osokin.

"Well, of course, you are a poet, and I've heard that you have written some beautiful poems. Why would you not read any of them when you came last time?"

"I never read in public. I mean, among people I don't know. It is enough for one single person to be—or to appear to be—out of harmony with my verses to make it impossible for me to read them. There is no sense in doing so because everything would be lost."

"And who disturbed you last time? I, perhaps?"

"No, not you," says Osokin, laughing, and as he looks at her he sees how her eyes and her whole face are changing. "The difficulty was that several of the people there seemed to be inhabitants of some other planet. Take your brother, for instance. I am very fond of him, but he is quite genuinely convinced that all these 'impressions from beyond' are simply pretentious nonsense; when as a matter of fact the earth need not exist at all for my verses. But, if I said this to him, he would think that I was deliberately talking nonsense from a desire to appear original."

"Yes, probably he would," says Zinaida. "I envy you your strength of character. I often feel myself that one cannot talk about everything with everyone, but I can't always restrain myself . . . Will you read your poems to me?"

"Some time later, perhaps," says Osokin. "In my verses there is always *very much of me*, therefore you must know *me* first. I think that is how it should be. I am very fond of poems of one line—some Roman poets wrote them—but it is difficult to understand these poems without knowing the men who wrote them."

For some time Osokin rows in silence.

"I too have known you for a long time," says Zinaida, "at least, I've heard about you."

"What have you heard about me?"

"I heard that you had a very interesting adventure when you were in the Military School and found yourself, as a result, somewhere in Askabad. Is that true?"

"Quite true, only it was still farther away," says Osokin laughing. "But that was a long time ago."

"Well, what of it? What has been will be again."

"I don't think the magician meant that," says Osokin, laughing again.

"Then what did he mean?"

"I think he meant that the future has already been, and that nothing really exists, that everything is a dream and a mirage. Sometimes I understand this very clearly. Don't you feel the unreality of all this?" Osokin makes a sweeping gesture with his hand. "The forest, the water, the sky—none of it exists, you know. There have been days when I felt that everything was becoming transparent, so to speak, and might disappear at any moment. Just like this: you see everything around you, you think that it exists; you shut your eyes, then you open them and there is nothing.

"Once, soon after I came to Paris, I went to Notre Dame and climbed the South Tower, where the public is not usually admitted, and spent the whole day there, on the top, quite alone. All the time I was improvising verses, and sometimes I wrote them down. I imagined in these verses that people had disappeared . . . Many years have passed away and I am looking down from the tower of Notre Dame onto an empty Paris, and the gargoyles are looking down with me . . . You understand, there are no people left, they have vanished long ago, two, three hundred years ago—The bridges are overgrown with grass, and some parts are beginning to fall down. The embankment is crumbling away, the asphalt is cracked, and green bushes and trees are growing in the crevices. The panes of the windows have been broken by the wind or have fallen out. And Notre Dame stands and recalls the past of Paris. The gargoyles talk to each other of all the things they have seen which will never be again; and suddenly they understand that there never has been anything, that they themselves do not exist, and that nothing exists. The moment they understand this, they see people and life again as it was before, and Paris becomes once more the ordinary Paris. But now it is clear to them that neither the people, nor their life—nor the cathedral or the gargoyles themselves really exist . . . I wrote down these verses, but later I lost them, so now they too do not exist."

Zinaida shudders as though she were cold.

"You make me feel that nothing exists," she says. "But how could you have lost those verses. Don't you remember them?"

"I remember nothing. I only remember that for a long time one of the gargoyles refused to speak, then said something strange and incomprehensible."

"But surely you know that those are not the real gargoyles? They never saw Esmeralda."

"So they say, but that makes no difference to me. After all, no one knows for certain. Personally, I don't believe that the eighteenth century could have made those gargoyles."

They are silent for some time. Then Zinaida begins to talk about Italy.

Osokin listens. Suddenly the thought flashes through his mind that soon they must go back, and he feels a strange pang at his heart. He wishes that this might never end; the slow movement along the river, the rocking of the boat, the lapping of the water, the conversation that passes from one subject to another. Involuntarily he feels that among other people and in other surroundings Zinaida will also be different, will again be a stranger—while here she is wonderfully near to him. It is so pleasant here on the river in the shadow of the trees. He wants to make her talk about herself.

"And did you have many admirers abroad?" he asks.

"Many," she answers laughingly, "but all of them unreal."

"And what is the difference between real and unreal admirers?"

"The real ones are those whom I also could admire, or in any case with whom I like to be, and not only those who admire me and want to be with me. Do you understand?"

"Maybe. So admirers are unreal if you don't want to see too much of them. Was it as bad as that?"

"Yes certainly. If you were a woman you would know what it means when you are proposed to. It's awfully unpleasant. A man doesn't know this feeling. Many girls like it, but I don't. You understand, you can even be quite friendly towards a man and have nothing against him. You can go riding with him, dance with him, even flirt a little . . . but from this he draws his own conclusions, and these do not please you at all. Then one fine day you notice that he has already made some plans about you and is only waiting for an opportunity to reveal them. Then a struggle begins between you and him. You do your utmost to prevent him from revealing these plans to you. Sometimes it can be very funny . . . The struggle goes on. Not every man has sufficient self-assurance or self-confidence to take no notice of you and go straight ahead. Most men have to be in a sentimental mood; without this they cannot speak. So you carefully avoid sentimental moods, and for a time you succeed. Sometimes, by taking the right tone in a conversation, you may ward off the danger. But sooner or later, at an unfortunate moment, you are caught and informed of all the splendid plans and intentions he has for you. Then comes the most unpleasant part. To begin with, some men are deeply and genuinely surprised if you dislike their projects; they simply cannot understand why this is so. It seems to them there is some misunderstanding that will disappear the moment they explain their ideas to you more clearly. So they begin to explain their plans to you. They honestly believe that you have not sufficiently realized how beautifully and how admirably they have thought it all out. At last, if you still refuse to accept with gratitude the magnanimous plans made for you, they bring up against you some words which you have completely forgotten and which meant something entirely different when you said them; and they insist that the idea was really your own, that you yourself suggested it and so on and so on. No, it's really terrible!"

"It looks as though you've had a great deal of practice. And you, were you always so cold yourself?"

"And why are you interested in that?"

"Because I understand one thing that only very few people understand," says Osokin.

"What is that?"

"I understand how difficult it is for a clever and interesting woman to meet a man with whom she can fall in love, and with whom it would be worth falling in love. In my opinion there are many more interesting women than interesting men, and I often think that, if I were a woman, it would be difficult for me to find a man in whom I could be interested."

"Why is that?"

"I don't know, but I have this feeling. Among all the men I know, there is not one in whom I could be interested if I were a woman. I even think sometimes that if I had a sister I should not want her to marry any of my friends or people I meet."

"How unusual that is," she says, laughing. "Men are generally so convinced of their superiority."

"But I am not. I consider that women belong to a higher caste than men. And it is easy to understand why. For thousands of years, women have been in a privileged position."

"In a privileged position! I can imagine what my two English friends would say to that. They are profoundly convinced that women have been enslaved by men and have only recently begun to win their freedom."

"Yes, I can imagine what your friends would say, but I still insist on my point: women occupy a privileged position in life. By this of course I mean women of the educated classes in more or less civilized countries. Consider only one thing. For thousands of years women have taken no active part in wars, and have rarely had anything to do with politics or Government service. In this way they have avoided the most fraudulent and criminal sides of life. This alone makes women more free than men. Of course, there are different kinds of women: and undoubtedly the modern woman does everything she can to lose her caste.

"But don't conclude from all this that I'm very enthusiastic about women as they are," Osokin adds, laughing. "I think they lack discernment. To their instinct has been entrusted an immense task—the task of selection. I don't mean this in any biological sense, but in a more aesthetic and moral sense. They perform this task badly because they content themselves with insignificant men. Woman's chief sin is that she is not sufficiently *exacting*, and often she is not exacting at all."

"I like many things that you say," says Zinaida, "though I must think more about them. Well, and what women have you met, exacting or not exacting?"

"I don't think I have ever met one sufficiently exacting," says Osokin.

"And would you like to meet one?"

"Very much."

"That pleases me," she says, "and I quite agree with you that women are not sufficiently exacting. They give themselves away too cheaply."

"Those are dangerous words," says Osokin, laughing again. "They can be too easily misinterpreted. You see, I am not speaking from the point of view of women's practical interests. If a woman is demanding *for herself*, it is merely vulgar—and of this kind of demanding there is more than enough no matter what form it may take. I am speaking about something quite different. Woman does not demand enough from man for *his own sake.*

"Has she not the right to demand a great deal for herself?"

"That is quite another question," says Osokin. "That is *life*. I was never interested in this."

They are silent as the boat drifts along slowly with the current towards the landing place. They walk back through the pine wood again, and as they come near to the house Osokin says good-bye. To his surprise, Zinaida says:"I shall be in town to-morrow: if you have nothing to do we might meet. Call at my brother's apartment about three, I shall have finished all I have to do by then."

Evening. Osokin is going home. He is sitting in a railway carriage, and he looks out of the window at the fields passing rapidly by; he smiles and feels unusually cheerful.

"God, what didn't we talk about!" he thinks. "She is a dear, and after all, just as I imagined her to be long ago. It's incredible how I knew her so well before and how different she appeared at our first meeting. I haven't talked for a long time as I did to-day. How wonderful it is that I shall see her to-morrow. Of course, nothing can come of it. In the winter, or at the latest in the early spring, I shall go away; but all the same it's a good thing that I've met the mythical Zinaida. Of no one woman have I dreamed so much as of her; and all these dreams came only from seeing photographs of her and hearing about her. That's very interesting. Well, we'll see how our meeting goes to-morrow. I liked her suggesting it herself. She is certainly a fascinating woman. She's as clever as Valerie, and has enough imagination for ten Loulous. Yes, it's a good thing that I've met her; at least it will be something to remember Moscow by . . ."

CHAPTER XXIV
THE INEVITABLE

TWO WEEKS LATER. Osokin is waiting for Zinaida in the park by the river. He walks up and down the path, smoking.

"How strange all this is," he says to himself. "I've never experienced anything like it. I don't know what it is—love, or something like that. I like to see her, I like to talk to her. I wait for her here every day like a schoolboy, and we go on the river. It would be hard for me now to miss a single day. Yet the first time I saw her I definitely did not like her, either her style or herself as a woman. Later, on the contrary, I began to like her very much. But in my attitude towards her there is nothing personal. It's unlike anything I've read or heard of, and it is so unlike me. At the same time, I know that these meetings can have no sequel. I must go away. That is inevitable. Nothing will come of my staying here. I like knowing Zinaida very much, but life will soon put an end to it. It's pure chance that I've been free these last two weeks— and with enough money to come here. But I don't in the least know what I shall do next week. Of course, she doesn't understand or realize it . . ."

He turns round and looks along the avenue.

"But why does she not come? It's already one o'clock and they have lunch at twelve. Well, in a year's time everything here will be just as it is now. It may be that she'll be walking along this same avenue—and I shall no longer be here. Where shall I be? It's difficult even to imagine."

A week later. Osokin and Zinaida are walking in the park. The path is already strewn with yellow leaves.

"Well, are you going to Australia soon?" asks Zinaida, looking at Osokin with a smile.

"You know I'm not going anywhere," answers Osokin.

Zinaida laughs and pulls him by the sleeve.

"I shall never forgive you," she says. "If only you knew how angry you made me with your Australia! Often, I simply wanted to hit you. Men are so awfully stupid sometimes. Surely a woman shows plainly that she is interested in a man if she is ready to see him every day; if she spends nearly all her time with him and invents different reasons for meeting him. And, in return for all this, I have been offered plans about Australia! Yes, my dear, you were delightful . . . But now, I want you to tell me about Australia."

"Darling," says Osokin, taking her hand, "you ought to understand how hard it was for me to say all that."

"If it was hard, why did you do it?"

"I thought it was inevitable. Circumstances had arranged themselves in such a way that I could not think of anything else; and it was decided long before I met you."

"Yes, but I have been imprudent enough to suppose that meeting me might have changed some of your plans. Evidently not; that hasn't even occurred to you. So at last I've had to take the trouble of explaining the position to you myself. What can you say in your defense?"

"I can't say anything," says Osokin.

"Well, but what about your circumstances? You said they made it imperative for you to go to Australia. Have they changed then?"

"It isn't that they have changed, they've simply lost all meaning. I don't believe I have ever felt nearer to the world of fairy tales than I do now—and when I feel that, it seems to me that everything will be different and not what I thought it would be."

"Well, let us suppose you are not going to Australia but will remain here. I'm interested to know whether I occupy any place in your plans or not?"

Osokin suddenly takes her in his arms and kisses her.

"Listen! Have you gone mad?" Zinaida tears herself away from him and arranges her hair. She is really angry and frightened. "We could be seen here at any moment."

"Let them see! I'll kiss you each time you mention Australia, I give you my word."

"How good of you! Yes, now you've become brave. Do you remember how it was a week ago? You were afraid to touch my hand. Of course, it is very easy for you to be brave now when I've done all the difficult part—begun to speak to you of myself and made you speak. Certainly, now you hold all the trumps. This is what always happens, and we women always pay for our frankness and candor. But I mean to punish you. When we get home, I shall go on talking about Australia, and to keep your word you'll be obliged to kiss me all the time." She laughs. "I can imagine what Mother's face will look like when you kiss me! And the lady with the little dog will also be there, and the proper young maidens of the locality who come to see me . . . Will you like that? You see how easy it is to catch you out and how much your promises are worth!"

Her eyes are sparkling with a thousand fires.

"That's the first thing. And now the second. I'm interested to know how long we might have gone on talking about poetry and New Art if I had not, one fine day, upset your good behavior. You men are usually supposed to be the stronger sex, but what would you do without us? Why do you look in my eyes? No, please don't show your courage, we are just coming to the houses . . . Let us talk seriously. I still want to know your plans. If you are not going to Australia, then what do you intend to do? Have you any plans or not? You see how frankly I put my questions."

Osokin glances at Zinaida; and he realizes that it has been very difficult for her to force herself to speak in this way, knowing that he will not speak himself. He realizes too that she is trying to make it easier for him to approach her, but also that she is embarrassed and wants to conceal her embarrassment by speaking to him as though she were joking. A feeling of great tenderness for her takes hold of him, but at the same time, a certain annoyance flares up in him. Why does she want to make him speak? She should understand that he *cannot* speak yet.

He looks at Zinaida again, and feels sorry for her and ashamed of his thoughts. How can she be blamed for anything? She only wants to help him. He is now filled with gratitude to her and a particularly deep regret that he cannot answer her as she expects. What prevents him? Cowardice, and a ridiculous kind of pride. He is afraid of finding himself in a false position. She is a rich girl and he has nothing. In fact, he is so penniless that only yesterday he pawned his overcoat in order to come here. And he has absolutely nothing to look forward to except what may come by chance. He has got off the beaten track. How will her mother and her brother regard him? In what position will he stand in relation to them? If she were alone . . . or if his tongue were not tied, if he were not afraid to speak, but could tell her straight out how things were . . . then perhaps, between them, they might find a way out.

Osokin feels that she wants him to speak, and yet he feels that he will say nothing. He knows this state of mind very well. There have been times before in his life when out of pride he has pretended not to notice that people wanted to help him and were making advances to him. In this way he has repelled them, and he has been aware of doing it. It is the same now. Well, this is his fate; he cannot act differently.

"Why do you say nothing?" asks Zinaida.

"Because I cannot say what I should like to say."

"What prevents you?"

"I need time. Just now everything is still going on as it did before. You know I wanted to go away and didn't much care what was happening here. Now I am not going, and I want to arrange my life here, but it needs time."

Zinaida frowns with displeasure. "I don't like time. You know I like to have things at once. If I am told that I must wait for something, I'm ready to give it up; it's already spoiled for me. You know this feeling? If I were offered a trip to the moon and then it appeared that I had to wait two years for it, I should give up any moon in the world. And you?"

"I quite understand that," says Osokin, "but perhaps I shall wait for the moon." He smiles and looks at her. "That is why I can say nothing now."

They are silent for some time. Osokin feels a pang at his heart. He knows that he has offended Zinaida and repulsed her, and at the same time he knows that he could not have spoken differently.

Zinaida is looking straight in front of her, her lips tightly pressed together. It seems to Osokin that now she is sorry she has spoken, and he is annoyed with himself and with everything.

"She ought to understand that our relationship cannot be like any ordinary one," he thinks. "Things can't be as they would have been with any other man. I am in an exceptional position; I can't even dress decently. When they move to town, she will want me to go everywhere with her. She has already spoken about it. Where am I to get the money for this? I only just manage to exist at present, and even that is difficult enough. No, something must happen or I really shall have to go away. So far, for some reason, fate has always come to my rescue at the last moment; we'll see what will happen this time. But perhaps I'm just a fool. Perhaps *she* is my fate. Perhaps I should just tell her everything quite simply, and discuss with her what to do. That is what she wants and what she is asking of me—and that is precisely what I cannot do. I repulse her in this way. I know it and can do nothing about it."

By now they are quite near to the house. Osokin has the feeling that in another half hour he would have spoken.

"Will you come in?" asks Zinaida.

"No, I'll see you to-morrow," says Osokin. "I don't want to speak to anyone but you to-day. You are not going anywhere?"

"I? No, nowhere," says Zinaida slowly, looking away as though she were thinking of something else. "I shall not be going anywhere for some time."

Osokin feels that she is annoyed and hurt by this talk. She seems troubled and sad. He bends towards her slightly. Somehow he feels madly, painfully sorry for her. He wants to say something tender and comforting, to kneel before her, to beg her forgiveness, to ask her not to leave him, not to believe in his coldness.

Her hands are cold. He kisses her fingers and her hand drops passively. They walk in silence to the garden gate.

"Of course, I know it's my fault," says Osokin to himself as he walks up and down the wooden platform at the station, waiting for his train. "A man has no right to be in such a helpless position as this. One cannot be a permanent failure. In such a case one ought to go away and disappear or start a new life in some way. It's no use knocking about here . . . Yes, I'd give a great deal now to have the money I lost at Bob's. But on the other hand, to be quite fair to destiny, if I had not lost my money, I should not yet have come to Moscow and should probably never have met Zinaida. So there was something good even in that . . . Well, all right, we'll see what will happen next. I must find work of some kind so that I can at least dress decently and have enough money for theatres and all such nonsense, otherwise I shall not be able to see Zinaida during the winter. It's a good thing they've decided to stay in the country for the whole of September.

"But how wonderfully nice she is! How beautiful it would be if I could tell her . . . Then it's true. I do feel something quite extraordinary about her. And she? Why does she like me? I can't understand it. She says she has never talked to anyone as she has to me. But how strange it is; I've never experienced anything like this. It is something quite new. And how necessary she has become to me. Why can I find no words when I am speaking to her? If she were here now, at this moment, I could tell her everything."

CHAPTER XXV
A WINTER'S DAY

A COLD, SUNNY WINTER DAY in Moscow. Osokin and Zinaida are walking along Tverskoi boulevard. Osokin is wearing a thin overcoat and a felt hat. They have been silent for a long time, then Zinaida begins to speak.

"I don't understand you. You say that you want to see me, that you always have so much to tell me; and it's true, we always have very much to tell each other. But why must we meet by stealth in the streets? Why can't you come to our house as everyone else does? I'm beginning to think that, for some reason, you don't want to attract attention to yourself and me. All this gives me the impression that you are afraid of someone, trying to conceal from someone that you are interested in me. To me this is strange. I realize that your finances are not in a very bright condition, but why don't you arrange them? It could be done so easily. You have a ridiculous kind of pride. Why won't you do what was suggested to you a short while ago? I know about it. You must forget for a time that you're a poet and take a job. It can easily be arranged. And then you will immediately have credit for whatever you want."

"Darling, you don't understand that it is quite impossible."

"Why is it impossible? Other people work. You could write poetry in the evenings. Surely you realize that you cannot live by writing poetry? Are there many people who understand your poems?"

Osokin laughs gaily.

"Oh, I must tell you an amusing story. The day before yesterday I went to that picnic with the Leontieffs because I thought you would be there. On the whole, it was very dull, although it was a wonderful day. It was cold and everything sparkled. The snow was fresh and soft on the fields, on the lake and on the pines. The sun was shining and everything glittered, especially when we drove out of the forest and the road stretched away down before us. You know, I had the impression that a huge white cat was lying on its back basking in the sun and purring. The best way to express such fleeting impressions is in poems of one line; for the more you leave to the imagination of the reader or the hearer, the better. So I put it all in one line:

The fluffy white belly of winter.

"How do you like it? Can you see a huge, fluffy, white cat?"

Zinaida cannot help laughing.

"It's very good," she says, "but I'm afraid that after reading that line every ordinary mortal will ask: 'And what comes next?' "

"Quite right, and that is how it should be. Only *next* is in the reader himself. If he doesn't see that, and wants to have everything given him, he had better subscribe to the 'Niva.' That is just what happened the other day; and that's what I wanted to tell you. I was rash enough to speak of my poetical experiment to my companions in the sleigh. It evoked great merriment. They started to pester me with this very question of what comes next. Then, as I didn't answer, they tried to compose a continuation. They began to look for rhymes— the most awful things—and generally, to amuse themselves. The others too; they all liked it. It became a sort of *petit jeu*, and everyone tried his wits."

Zinaida glances at him.

"Tell me the truth, was this not unpleasant for you?"

"There was nothing unpleasant at the beginning. I laughed quite honestly with them and quite shared their point of view—because really they cannot look at it in any other way. But after a while I began to feel angry with myself for having started the talk, and in order to stop it I made several impromptu verses about them. They didn't know whether to laugh or to be offended. They roared with laughter when they repeated my verses to one another, but they really felt very foolish."

"And that amuses you?" asks Zinaida, with a slight grimace.

"No, not particularly. It was silly of me to begin talking about my verses, but I was bored. I was sorry you were not there."

"And I am not sorry at all," says Zinaida. "You were gay enough without me." She looks straight in front of her and Osokin glances at her in surprise.

"I don't understand," he thinks. "What was it she didn't like? Certainly not what I told her; but something has displeased her."

Osokin says something else to her, but she listens absently and continues with her own thoughts.

"We've wandered away from what we were talking about before," she says. "You needn't justify yourself. I don't mind your enjoying yourself, but to me it is strange that you never have any time for me and that something always prevents you from coming to our house. I am only trying to understand it. I don't know why you refuse to consider the job that Misha mentioned to you. You will be given well paid work, and if you like you can look on it as temporary."

Osokin glances at her again and for a moment wants to agree with everything she says.

"You're quite right," he says, "and I will think about it seriously. But try to understand that, for me, it would be just as strange to become a *Tchinovnik** as, for instance, to join a revolutionary party—that also was suggested to me not long ago—and print pamphlets in cellars and agitate among 'conscious workmen.' I cannot imagine myself a 'comrade.' Thank God, I saw enough of them abroad."

* A civil servant.

"You know," he continues, without noticing Zinaida's frown of displeasure, "once when I was in Paris, I was invited to an 'evening' arranged by one of these 'parties' or 'groups.' They just talked and talked: how bad everything was, how miserable everybody was, and how beautiful everything would be if there were no police, no Cossacks and no General Governors . . . But when it came to having tea, it transpired that the members of the committee had eaten all the cakes and oranges, and drunk all the tea! So there was nothing left for the rest of us."

Zinaida becomes exasperated.

"I am not interested in your friends, either in Paris or in Moscow," she says impatiently. "What have these two things in common? Those 'parties' are sheer lunacy or worse. And you know that quite well yourself. What I am speaking about is a perfectly normal thing. You would be working for yourself and also for the sake of being with me."

For some time they walk in silence.

" 'Darling Zulu lady,' " thinks Osokin, in the words of a Petersburg writer he particularly likes. "How beautifully she finished with revolution! She doesn't realize for a second that there are people who die for this idea. And the funniest thing is that, fundamentally, she is quite right. These people are good for nothing. They will probably cause a great deal of harm, but they will never create anything. Some of them are very nice people, quite sincere and terribly unselfish. But those will perish. Only scoundrels will survive."

Yet, at the same time, Osokin feels a little uneasy, and he looks at Zinaida with a kind of question in his glance. The Government, and all that belongs to it, has become so unpopular in the last twenty years that, like all the 'intelligentsia' he has a certain almost obligatory sympathy towards any anti-government attitude or activity; and he cannot understand why Zinaida does not share his feeling in this respect.

Osokin himself does not believe in the necessity or advantage of a revolution in Russia. He can see the possibility of a different way, if only those in responsible positions would not be so childishly selfish and stupid. There is still much that is good in the people. And he dislikes 'the party public' as he calls them, and their presumptuous talk, even more than he dislikes the arrogance of official Russia. Nevertheless Zinaida's attitude jars on him slightly and somehow lowers her in his eyes, although he does not like to feel this.

An extraordinary vivid picture passes through his mind.

He was a boy of twelve or thirteen, in the second or third form at school. One Saturday afternoon he was walking down Petrovka from Kuznetsky Most, going to buy a pair of kid gloves at Babushkin's with some money he had received for the New Year. Suddenly in this narrow old-fashioned street with low houses and a church on the corner—but with the best and most expensive shops in Moscow and especially the large flower shops—there appeared a low, broad, peasant's sledge with a small piebald horse, driven by a peasant in a sheepskin coat and a fur cap. In the sledge, between two soldiers with drawn swords, was sitting, or kneeling, a most extraordinary-looking man, dressed in a convict's yellow coat and small yellow cap. His hands were tightly clenched in front of him with chains hanging from the wrists. His thin, emaciated face, with a thin black beard, which at once reminded Osokin of the face of John the Baptist in Ivanoff's picture, was raised up. His head, with its flowing black hair, was thrown back, and the gaze of his strange, unseeing eyes seemed to pass high over the street with its gay crowd, quickly moving sledges, and shining carriages with beautiful horses. This vision lasted only a few moments. The sledge disappeared among the traffic . . .

Osokin remembers how he stopped and looked after the sledge. "Where are they taking him?" he asked himself. "Evidently to the law courts. They will send him to Siberia . . . Who is he? What has he done?"—and he felt terribly afflicted and suddenly lost interest in everything.

He feels that Zinaida would never understand this vision,

she would never feel the incomprehensible side of it. For her it would be, quite seriously and in a grown-up way, only 'lunacy or worse.'

"I feel that something stands between us," says Zinaida, breaking into Osokin's thoughts. "I don't want to think anything, I don't want to suppose anything, but I *feel* it. Perhaps you are right not to speak of it to me."

"Darling, there is nothing for me to speak about."

"Perhaps not, but this is how I feel," repeats Zinaida. "I believe there is something which is gradually affecting me. I am not the same towards you as I was in the summer. You mustn't be offended. I still have a great deal of feeling for you, but it's not what it was. I'm a little afraid of you—afraid of coming too near to you and then finding that I am unnecessary, or that I am interfering with something or with someone. Don't argue with me. I know what you will say, but I am telling you how *I* feel about it. And I'm afraid it will become worse as time goes on. Please understand that I am very sorry about it. I liked our meetings very much, and I liked my feeling for you. I've never had such an attitude towards anyone before. I even wanted to look after you, to think about your life. I mean all this quite seriously; and it's not like me at all. I'm such an egoist and I never concern myself about anyone as a rule. Try to understand that I liked the fact that, in relation to you, I was becoming different, such as I'd never been before . . . But you force me to remain as I was, and to have the same attitude towards you as I have to everyone else. Well, so be it; only, I shall be sorry if my feeling for you disappears altogether. Well, now it is time to go home— it was time long ago. To-morrow, as you suggested, we may go to the Roumiantsevsky Museum. I must confess that I've never been there, and you say there are interesting pictures. Well, you can meet me in the same place, at the same time as to-day. But think about what I have said to you. Don't argue, just think . . ."

Osokin walks home.

"I understand nothing," he says to himself. "Why is it all turning out like this? I like her, I like to be with her, I would do anything for her. I've never experienced anything like it in all my life. Every night I walk twice, sometimes several times, past the house where she lives, and it gives me enormous pleasure just to see the windows of her room.

"At the same time, everything is happening in the wrong way, and I am doing all the wrong things. I never tell her what I ought to tell her, or what I think and feel. Why? It's as though there were a mist around me, or as though I were tied and forced to act in this way and in no other. And then, why am I, all of a sudden, so disgusted at the thought of that job? When I first came to Moscow I should have grasped it with both hands had it been offered to me. But now such deadly boredom takes hold of me at the very thought of this employment that I cannot raise a finger to do anything about it. I invent all kinds of explanations for Zinaida—and I see that she does not believe me.

"But seriously speaking, how can I accept help from her relatives or friends? That is absolutely impossible. At the same time, I realize that I'm spoiling everything for myself by my own actions. She doesn't understand me; I seem odd to her. If only she could understand what I feel about her and how awfully difficult it is for me! I worry all the time and can find no way out. Ways that would be simple and natural for other people are, for some reason, impossible and quite closed for me. Can it really be that she will change towards me? Is there anything I can do? Why is there this terribly cold feeling in me as though I already knew and felt that something disastrous and final is bound to happen as it has always happened before?"

CHAPTER XXVI
THE TURN OF THE WHEEL

ON THE SCREEN a scene at Kursk Station in Moscow.

A bright April day of 1902. A group of friends who came to see Zinaida Krutitsky and her mother off to the Crimea stand by the sleeping car.

Among them is Osokin.

Osokin is visibly agitated although he tries not to show it. Zinaida is talking to her brother, a young officer in the uniform of one of the Grenadier regiments, and two girls. Then she turns to Osokin and walks aside with him.

"I am going to miss you very much," she says. "It's a pity you cannot come with us. Though it seems to me that you don't particularly want to, otherwise you would come. You don't want to do anything for me. Your staying behind makes all that we have talked about seem ridiculous and futile. But I am tired of arguing with you. You must do as you like."

Osokin becomes more and more troubled, but he tries to control himself and says with an effort:

"I can't come at present. But I shall come later, I promise you. You cannot imagine how hard it is for me to stay here."

"No, I cannot imagine it, and I don't believe it," says Zinaida quickly. "When a man wants anything as strongly as you say you do, he acts. I am sure you are in love with one of your pupils here—some nice poetical girl who studies fencing. Confess!" She laughs.

Zinaida's words and tone hurt Osokin very deeply. He begins to speak but stops himself, then says: "You know that is not true; you know I am all yours."

"How am I to know?" says Zinaida with a surprised air. "You are always busy. You always refuse to come to see us.

You never have any time for me. And now I should so much like you to come with us. We should be together for two whole days. Just think how pleasant the journey would be!"

She throws a quick glance at Osokin.

"And afterwards, there in the Crimea, we would ride together and we would sail far out to sea. You would read me your poems. And now I shall be bored." She frowns and turns away.

Osokin tries to reply, but finding nothing to say, he stands biting his lips.

"I shall come later," he repeats.

"Come when you like," says Zinaida indifferently, "but this chance is lost already. I shall be bored travelling alone. Mother is a very pleasant travelling companion, but that is not what I want. Thank God, I have seen one man I know, evidently going by this train. He may amuse me on the way."

Osokin again begins to speak, but Zinaida continues:

"I'm only interested in the present. What do I care for what may happen in the future? You don't realize this. You can live in the future, I cannot."

"I understand it all," says Osokin, "and it's very hard for me—yet I cannot help it. But will you remember what I asked you?"

"Yes, I shall remember, and I'll write to you. But I don't like writing letters. Don't expect many; come soon instead. I shall wait a month for you, two months—after that I will not wait any more. Well, let us go. Mother is looking for me."

They rejoin the group by the sleeping-car.

Osokin and Michail Krutitsky walk towards the station exit.

"What is the matter, Vanya?" says the latter. "You don't look very cheerful."

Osokin is not in a mood for talking.

"I'm all right," he says, "but I am sick of Moscow. I too should like to go away somewhere."

They come out towards the large asphalt square in front of the station. Krutitsky shakes hands with Osokin, walks down the steps, hails a carriage and drives off.

Osokin stands for a long time looking after him.

"There are times when it seems to me that I remember something," he says to himself slowly, "and others when it seems that I have forgotten something very important. I feel as though all this happened before in the past. But when? I don't know. How strange!"

Then he looks round like a man waking up.

"Now she has gone and I am here alone. Only to think that I might be travelling with her at this very moment! That would be all I could wish for at present. To go south, to the sunshine, and to be with her for two whole days. Then later on, to see her every day . . . and the sea and the mountains . . . But instead of that I stay here. And she doesn't even understand why I don't go. She doesn't realize that at the present moment I have exactly thirty kopecks in my pocket. And if she did, it would make it no easier for me."

He looks back once more at the entrance to the station hall, then with bent head goes down the steps to the square.

Three months later at Osokin's lodgings. A large room which is rented furnished. Rather poor surroundings. An iron bedstead with a grey blanket, a wash-stand, a chest of drawers, a small writing table, an open bookcase. On the wall, portraits of Shakespeare and Pushkin and some foils and masks.

Osokin, looking very perturbed and irritated, is walking up and down the room. He flings aside a chair that is in his way. Then he goes to the table, takes from the drawer three letters in long narrow grey envelopes, reads them one after another and puts them back.

First letter. Thank you for your letters and your verses. They are delightful. Only, I should like to know to whom they refer—not to me I am sure, otherwise you would be here.

Second letter. You still remember me? Really, it often seems to me that you write from habit, or from a strange sense of duty you have invented for yourself.

Third letter. I remember everything I said. The two months are coming to an end. Don't try to justify yourself or to explain. That you have no money, I know, but I have never asked for it. There are people living here who are much poorer than you.

Osokin walks about the room, then pauses near the table and says aloud:

"And she writes no more. The last letter came a month ago. And I write to her every day."

There is a knock at the door. Osokin's friend Stoupitsyn, a young doctor, walks into the room. He shakes hands with Osokin and sits down at the table in his overcoat.

"What is the matter with you? You're looking very ill."

He comes quickly to Osokin and with mock seriousness tries to feel his pulse. Osokin smiles and waves him away, but the next moment a shadow crosses his face.

"Everything is rotten, Volodya," he says. "I can't express it clearly to you, but I feel as though I had cut myself off from life. All you other people are moving on while I am standing still. It looks as though I had wanted to shape my life in my own way, but had only succeeded in breaking it in pieces. The rest of you are going along by the ordinary ways. You have your life now and a future ahead of you. I tried to climb over all the fences and the result is that I have nothing now and nothing for the future. If only I could begin again from the beginning! I know now that I should do everything differently. I should not rebel in the same way against life and everything it offered me. I know now that one must first submit to life before one can conquer it. I have had so many chances, and so many times everything has turned in my favor. But now there is nothing left."

"You exaggerate," says Stoupitsyn. What difference is there between you and the rest of us? Life is not particularly pleasant for anyone. But why, has anything especially disagreeable happened to you?"

"Nothing has happened to me, only I feel out of life."

There is another knock at the door. Osokin's landlord, a retired civil servant, comes in. He is slightly drunk and extremely affable and talkative, but Osokin is afraid he will ask for his rent and tries to get rid of him. When the landlord has gone, Osokin, with a look of disgust on his face, waves his hand towards the door.

"You see, the whole of life is a petty struggle with petty difficulties like that," he says. "What are you doing this evening?"

They talk for some time. Osokin has always felt that Stoupitsyn understands him better than many of his other friends, and he likes to talk with him. He tries to explain his state of mind and his thoughts without mentioning Zinaida. But he feels that this time Stoupitsyn fails to understand him and argues only against his words.

After some time Stoupitsyn gets up, pats Osokin on the shoulder, takes the book for which he came and leaves.

Osokin also prepares to go out. Then he walks up to the table and stands there in his hat and coat, lost in thought.

"Everything would have been different," he says, "if I could have gone to the Crimea. And after all why didn't I go? I could at least have got there, and once there, what would anything else have mattered? Perhaps I could have found some work. But how on earth could one live at Yalta without money? Horses, boats, cafés, tips—all that means money. And one has to dress decently. I could not have gone there in the same clothes I wear here. All these things are only trifles, but when these same trifles are put together . . . And she doesn't understand that I could not live there. She thinks that I don't want to come, or that something keeps me here. . . . Will there really be no letter again today?"

Osokin goes to inquire whether there are any letters for him at the General Post Office, where he had asked Zinaida to write to him. There are no letters. As he comes out, he runs into a man in a dark blue overcoat.

Osokin stops and follows the man with his eyes.

"Who is that man? Where have I seen him? The face is very familiar. I even know that overcoat."

Lost in thought, he walks on. At the corner of the street he stops to allow an open carriage with a pair of horses to pass him. In the carriage are a man and two ladies whom he has met at Krutitsky's house. Osokin half raises his hand to take off his hat, but they do not see him. He laughs and walks on.

At the next corner he runs into Michail Krutitsky. The latter stops and taking Osokin's arm, walks along with him, saying:

"Have you heard the news? My sister is going to be married to Colonel Minsky. The wedding will be at Yalta, and afterwards they mean to go to Constantinople and from there to Greece. I'm going to the Crimea in a few days. Have you any message?"

Osokin laughs and shakes hands with him, and answers in a cheerful voice: "Yes, give her my greetings and congratulations."

Krutitsky says something else, laughs and walks away.

Osokin says good-bye to him with a smiling face. But after they have parted, his face changes. He walks on for some time, then stops and stands looking down the street taking no notice of the passers-by.

"Well, so that is what it means," he says to himself. "Now everything is clear to me. But what ought I to do? Go there and challenge Minsky to a duel? But why? It was evidently all decided beforehand, and I was wanted just for amusement. What a good thing I didn't go there. No, that's vile of me! I have no right to think that and it's not true. All this has happened because I did not go. But I certainly shall not go now, and I won't do anything. She has chosen. What right have I to be dissatisfied? After all, what can I offer her? Could I take her to Greece?"

He walks on, then stops again and continues to talk to himself.

"But it seems to me that she really felt something for me. And how we talked together! There was no one else in the world to whom I could talk in that way. She is so extraordinary! And Minsky is ordinary among the ordinary; a staff-colonel, and he reads the 'Novoe Vremya.' But quite soon he will be a man of standing—and I am not even recognized by her friends in the street."

"No, I cannot . . . I must either go somewhere or . . . I cannot stay here."

Evening. Osokin in his room. He is writing a letter to Zinaida Krutitsky, but tears up sheet after sheet and begins afresh. From time to time he jumps up and walks about the room. Then he begins to write again. At last he throws down the pen and falls back in his chair, exhausted.

"I can't write any more," he says to himself. "I have written to her for whole days and whole nights. Now I feel as though something were broken in me. If none of my other letters said anything to her, this one will say nothing. I cannot . . ."

He rises slowly and, moving like a blind man, takes a revolver and cartridges from the drawer of the table, loads the revolver and puts it in his pocket. Then he takes his hat and coat, turns out the lamp and goes out.

CHAPTER XXVII
ON THE THRESHOLD

OSOKIN IS AT THE MAGICIAN'S HOUSE.

The magician, the same bent old man with a penetrating glance, dressed all in black, with a thin Persian stick inlaid with turquoise in his hand, sits with Osokin near the fire.

The same large, strangely furnished room, with its carpets, brocades, bookcases and bronze figures of Indian gods. The statue of Kwan-Yin in a recess, the big celestial globe on a red lacquered stand, the hourglass on the small ivory table near the magician's chair, and the big black Siberian cat sleeping on the back of the chair.

Osokin is gloomy. He smokes a cigar and says nothing. At a moment when he is particularly deep in thought the magician speaks.

"My dear friend, you knew it before."

Osokin starts and looks at him.

"How do you know what I am thinking?"

"I always know what you are thinking."

Osokin bows his head and stares at the carpet.

"Yes, I know it cannot be helped *now*," he says. "But if only I could bring back a few years of this miserable time which does not even exist, as you yourself always say. If only I could get back all the chances which life offered me and which I threw away. If only I could do things differently . . ." But as he says the words he suddenly feels afraid, he does not know why.

He stops and looks in perplexity at the magician. Then he glances round him.

"What a strange sensation," he says to himself. "Has all this happened before? It seemed to me just now that at some other time I have sat here. Everything was exactly the same, and I was saying the same words."

He looks inquiringly at the magician.

The magician returns his look, laughs quietly and nods.

"Everything has been before," he says, "and everything can be brought back, everything. But even that will not help."

Osokin finds himself shivering. What does it all mean? He came to the magician with a definite idea in his mind but now it eludes him, and he cannot put it in words. He must remember what it was, he must explain it to the magician. Why does this stupid fear paralyze him?

He throws his cigar into the fire, rises from his chair and paces up and down the room.

The old man sits watching him, nodding his head and smiling. There is amusement and irony in his look—not an unsympathetic irony, but one full of understanding, of compassion and pity, as though he would like to help but cannot.

Osokin stops in front of him and says like a man in a trance:

"I must go back. Then I shall change everything. I cannot go on living like this. We do absurd things because we do not know what lies ahead of us. If only we could know! If only we could see a little way ahead!

He walks up and down the room, then again stops in front of the magician.

"Listen," he says, "can't your magic do this for me? Can't you send me back? I have been thinking about it for a long time, and to-day, when I heard about Zinaida, I felt that this was the only thing left for me. Send me back, I shall do everything differently. I shall live in a new way and I shall be prepared for meeting Zinaida when the time comes. But I must remember everything, you understand, I must preserve all my experience and knowledge of life. I must remember that I have come back and not forget what I have come back for . . . ."

He stops.

"God, what am I saying? I said the very same thing *then*."

He looks at the magician.

The old man smiles and nods.

"I can carry out your wish," he says, "but it will not be of any use; it will not make things any better for you."

Osokin throws himself into an armchair and holds his head in his hands.

"Tell me," he says, "is it true that I have already been here with you before?"

"It is true," says the magician.

"And I asked you the same thing?"

"You did."

"And shall I come again?"

"That is not so certain. You may want to come, but you may not be able to. There are many sides to these problems which you do not know yet. You may meet quite unexpected difficulties. One thing only I can say for certain. Circumstances may change, but there is not the slightest possibility of doubt that you yourself will arrive at the same decision. In that there can be no difference and no change."

"But this is simply turning round on a wheel!" says Osokin. "It is a trap!"

The old man smiles.

"My dear friend," he says, "this trap is called life. If you want to repeat the experiment once more, I am at your service. But I warn you, you will change nothing; you can only make things worse."

"Even if I remember everything?"

"Even if you remember everything. First, because you will not retain this memory for long. It will be too painful, and you yourself will want to get rid of it and forget. And then you will forget. Second, even if you remember, it will not help you. You will remember and still continue to do the same things."

"But this is horrible," says Osokin. "Is there no way out?"

A nervous trembling takes hold of him so that again he

cannot speak. There is the cold of the grave in this thought. He feels that this is the fear of the inevitable, fear of himself, of that self from which there is no escape . . . He will be the same and everything will be the same.

At this moment, Osokin understands that if he goes back as he is everything will indeed go in the same way as before. He clearly remembers all those chains of events at school and afterwards, when everything happened as if by clockwork, as in a machine the movement of one wheel makes another wheel move. But at the same time he feels that he cannot accept things as they are now, cannot resign himself to the loss of Zinaida and to the thought that everything is his own fault.

Osokin and the magician are both silent.

"What am I to do then?" says Osokin at last almost in a whisper.

There is a long pause.

"My dear friend," says the magician, breaking the silence, "those are the first sensible words I have heard from you since the beginning of our acquaintance.

"You ask what you are to do. Listen to me attentively. What I am going to say to you is said to a man only once in his life, and even so only to very few men. If a man fails to understand, that is his own fault; it is not repeated. You come here, you complain, and you ask for a miracle. And, when I can, I do what you ask, because I sincerely wish to help you. But nothing comes of it. Try now to understand why nothing comes of it and why I am powerless to help you. Understand that I can carry out only your wishes, only what you ask for. I cannot give you anything on my own initiative. This is the law. Even what I am saying now I am able to say only because you have asked me what you are to do. If you had not asked, I could not have spoken.

"I can add something more to that. If you go back now, everything will be the same as before or worse. For instance, you may not meet me. You must understand that chances are limited; no one has unlimited chances. And you never know when you have used your last chance. On the other hand, if you go on living perhaps something can be changed sufficiently to enable you to start differently the next time."

"Is it worth while living for this?"

"That is your affair. You have to decide for youself. But remember one thing, if you go back as blind as you are now, you will do the same things again and a repetition of all that happened before is inevitable. You will not escape from the wheel ; everything will go on as before. You ask me what you are to do. I answer: *live*. It is your only chance.

"If you think carefully, you will find in my words all that you need. But if you still want to go back and begin again I will send you back even to the day of your birth, if you like. But I warn you that you will come here again—if you can. Now decide."

Osokin sits motionless in the armchair. There is another long silence.

Scenes and pictures of his life again pass before him: school —Mother—Paris—Zinaida. God, how many possibilities he has had and lost one after another! And life kept closing in on him until finally he found himself in a narrow tunnel with no way out. But suppose a way out really exists? Why does the magician insist that he should live? And what is the sense in going back if he is bound to come to the same point again, or perhaps to something even worse? What does the magician mean by this? What could be worse?

"When I first began to understand that everything repeats and returns," says Osokin to himself "it seemed to me an interesting adventure. But now it frightens me, and I feel I must do everything possible to postpone this experience. The adventure which attracted me lies in quite a different direction. Which direction I don't know yet. But I must find it, before I can risk returning."

At last Osokin looks up.

"I will live," he says. "You are right. I still cannot understand anything, but I do see that to start all this again is not a way out."

The magician looks at Osokin for a long time as though trying to penetrate into his mind.

"Now that you have said that you are going to live," he says at last, "I can tell you more. But first I want to ask you, do you think you know your Zinaida well?"

Osokin looks up in astonishment.

"I think I do," he says, "but what do you mean?"

The old man smiles again.

"If you know her well, how could you believe that she would marry Minsky?"

"How could I believe ... ? She said that she would not wait any longer for me. And I could not go. Then I met Krutitsky and he told me ..."

Osokin stops and is suddenly seized by a strange and wonderful feeling of hope, of more than hope—the expectation of a miracle.

Why does the magician speak about it?

"I could not tell you this before," continues the magician, "because I may not say anything that can influence your decisions. But now I can tell you that to-day Colonel Minsky passed through Moscow on his way to Petersburg. Zinaida broke off the engagement three days before the wedding. Besides, she never intended to marry him. Only you could fail to understand that."

Osokin sits with a bewildered expression on his face.

"Then she is not going to be married," he says as though he does not understand what he is saying. "But then why ... ?"

He looks at the magician as though he were seeing him for the first time.

"But why did you not tell me before?"

"Because you never asked. You accepted it as a fact and came to me with a ready-made decision. I cannot argue against ready-made decisions."

Osokin scarcely hears what the magician is saying.

"God, what an idiot I have been," he says to himself. "How could I have believed it? Of course, all this is nothing but her usual acting. She needed Minsky just for amusement, up to a certain point but not further. Of course it is clear to me that she would never have married him. How could I misunderstand her so much?"

Pictures of the last few months pass before him. He sees clearly how he has shut himself up in his pride and obstinacy. Of course he should have gone with Zinaida at all costs. Now, naturally, everything will be different.

Dozens of plans begin to form in his head. He sees himself in the train. Wheels are rattling. He is on his way to the Crimea. He will see Zinaida. After all, things can be arranged somehow.

The magician is speaking.

At first Osokin does not hear.

"Nothing will change," says the magician.

"What do you mean by saying that nothing will change?" says Osokin. "Everything has changed already."

The magician shakes his head and smiles.

"My dear friend, once more you deceive yourself. Nothing has changed. Everything is exactly the same as it has been up to now, and everything will remain the same. Nothing could change and nothing will change.

"*The wind returneth again according to his circuits ... The thing that has been, it is that which shall be; and that which is done is that which shall be done.*"

"And nothing can be changed?" says Osokin.

"I never said that nothing can be changed. I said that you cannot change anything, and that nothing will change by itself. I have already told you that in order to change anything you must first change yourself. And this is much more difficult than you think. It requires constant effort for a long time and much knowledge. You are incapable of such effort and you do not even know how to start. No one is capable of it by himself. People always repeat the same mistakes. At first they simply do not know that they move in a circle; and if they hear about this idea, they refuse to believe it. Later, if they begin to see the truth of it and accept it, they think that this is all that is necessary; they become fully convinced that now they know all they need to know and that they can change everything. And immediately they find charlatans who assure them that everything is very easy and simple. This is the greatest illusion of all. In this way men lose the chances which they have acquired through much suffering and sometimes even through great effort.

"You must remember that one may know many things and be unable to change anything, because changing requires different knowledge and also something which you do not possess."

"What is the thing we do not possess?"

"This question is very characteristic of you. Like everyone else, you think that you can know everything, when in fact you cannot know anything and cannot understand anything. How can I tell you what it is if it does not exist for you?"

Osokin is silent.

Yes, he feels that the magician is right. He cannot change anything. After his moment of exhilaration he is seized by fear and anguish. He will again do the same absurd things, he will again lose Zinaida.

"Then, what is required to make things begin to change?" he asks. And he expects the magician to answer with one of those probably very clever but, for him, almost meaningless phrases, such as: when you are different, everything else will be different.

But the magician says something that Osokin has not anticipated.

"You must realize," says the magician, "that you yourself can change nothing and that you must seek help. And it must be a very deep realization, because to realize to-day and forget to-morrow is not sufficient. One must live with this realization."

"But what does it mean to 'live with this realization'?" asks Osokin. "And who can help me?"

"*I* can help you," says the magician, "and to live with this realization means to sacrifice something big for it, not only once, but to go on making sacrifices until you get what you want."

"You speak in riddles," says Osokin. "What can I sacrifice? I have nothing."

"Everyone has something to sacrifice," says the magician, "except those who cannot be helped. But of course it is impossible to say beforehand what one may get for one's sacrifice. Do you remember the man who had to work seven years to win a wife, and in the end they gave him the wrong sister? He had to work another seven years. This often happens."

Osokin is silent. Something unpleasant stirs in him. What does the old man want from him?

"What I am saying seems strange to you," says the magician, "because you have never thought about these things in the right way. Besides, thinking by itself will not help. Here again, one must know. And in order to know, one must learn; and in order to learn, one must make sacrifices. Nothing can be acquired without sacrifice. This is the thing you do not understand, and until you understand it, nothing can be done. Had I wanted to give you, without any sacrifice on your part, everything you might wish, I could not have done it.

"A man can be given only what he can use; and he can use only that for which he has sacrificed something. This is the law of human nature. So if a man wants to get help to acquire important knowledge or new powers, he must sacrifice other things important to him at the moment. Moreover, he can only get as much as he has given up for it. There are additional difficulties due to his state. He cannot know exactly what he may get, but if he realizes the hopelessness of his position, he will agree to make sacrifices, even without knowing. And he will be glad to do so, because only in this way can he acquire the possibility of gaining something new or of changing himself; for if he does not sacrifice anything, then everything will remain the same for him or even become worse."

"Are there no other ways?" asks Osokin.

"You mean ways in which no sacrifices are necessary? No, there are no such ways, and you do not understand what you are asking. You cannot have results without causes. By your sacrifice you create causes. There are different ways, but they differ only in the form, magnitude and finality of the sacrifice. In most cases, one has to give up everything at once and expect nothing.

"There is a dervish song which goes like this:

> *Through four renunciations*
> *Ascend to perfection.*
> *Leave life without regret.*
> *Expect no reward in heaven.*

"Do you understand what that means? Most people can go only by this way or by one of the similar ways. But here, now, you are in a different position. You can talk with me. You can know what you have to give up and what you may get for it."

"How can I know what I can get? And how shall I know what I have to give up?"

"You can know what you may get through the realization of what it is you want. For some very complicated reasons which are all in yourself, you happen to have guessed a very great secret which people generally do not know. By itself your guess is useless because you cannot apply it to anything. But the fact that you know this secret opens certain doors for you. You know that everything repeats again and again. There have been other people who made the same discovery but they could make nothing more of it. If you could change something in yourself, you would be able to use this knowledge for your own advantage. So, you see, you do know what you want and what you may get.

"Now the question of what to sacrifice and how to sacrifice. You say you have nothing. Not quite. You have your life. So you can sacrifice your life. It is a very small price to pay since you meant to throw it away in any case. Instead of that, give me your life and I will see what can be made of you. I will even make it easier for you. I shall not require the whole of your life. Twenty, even fifteen years will be sufficient. But during these years you must belong to me—I mean, you must do everything I tell you without evasions and excuses. If you keep your side of the bargain, I shall keep mine. When this time is over you will be able to use your knowledge for yourself. It is your good luck that you can be useful to me just now—not at once, certainly, but I can wait if there is anything to wait for. So now you know what you have to sacrifice.

"There is something else which may be said. People who make the same guess that you have made have certain advantages and certain disadvantages in comparison with other people who guess nothing. Their advantage is that they can be taught what other people cannot be taught, and their disadvantage is that, for them, time becomes very limited. An ordinary man can turn round and round on the wheel and nothing happens to him until he finally disappears.

"Again, there are many things you do not know about this; but you must understand that in the course of time even the position of the stars in relation to one another changes—and men depend on the stars much more than they realize though not in the same way as they think, if they think about it at all. Nothing remains the same in time. But a man who has begun to guess the great secret must make use of it, otherwise it turns against him. It is not a safe secret. When one has become aware of it, one must go on or one will go down. When one finds the secret or hears about it, one has only two or three, or in any case only a few more lives.

"You must understand that, for reasons of my own, I am interested in such people in the same way as I am interested in you. But I can offer my help only at one particular moment and only once. If my help is not accepted, a man may not find me next time. It may sound strange to you, but the fact is that sometimes I see people who would like to come to me, walking along this street, but they cannot find my house. That is why I told you before that you may want to come to me again but not be able to."

"What happens to those people who cannot find your house?"

"Oh, they have other possibilities, but you must understand that every possibility is always more difficult than the preceding one; there is less and less time. If those people do not find new guidance and new help very soon, their lives begin to go down, and after some time they cease to be born and are replaced by other people. You must understand that they become useless, sometimes dangerous, because they know the great secret and remember many things; but all that they know, they understand in the wrong way. And in any case, if they have not used their chances before, then each time their possibilities become fewer.

"Now you must think about yourself. Fifteen years seem a long time to you because you are still very young. Later you will see that it is a very short time, especially when you realize what you can get for it. So go home and think. When you have understood and put in the right order everything I have said, you may come here and tell me what you have decided.

"I can only add one thing more. Like everyone else, you think that there are different ways of doing the same thing. You have to learn to understand that there is always only one way of doing a thing; there can never be two ways. But you will not come to this easily. For a long time you will have a great deal of inner argument. All this has to be destroyed. Only then will you be ready for real work. And understand another thing: only when you are useful to me will you be useful to yourself.

"I must also warn you that there are many dangers on the way, dangers about which you have never heard—or heard quite wrongly. A long time ago I met a very disagreeable gentleman who is sometimes pictured with horns and hoofs. He is not so big as some people make him out to be, but his chief occupation in life is to hinder the development of people who have guessed the great secret. And my occupation is to hinder him. So you must understand that very powerful forces will be opposed to you and you will be alone, always alone. Remember this.

"Now go, and come back when you have decided. Take as much time as you like, but I advise you not to delay too long."

CHAPTER XXVIII
CONCLUSION

OUT IN THE STREET Osokin walks for a long time without looking where he is going, and trying not to think. Then he sits down on a bench on some remote boulevard and remains motionless, without thoughts . . . But gradually all that has happened comes back to him.

"I must come to some decision," he says to himself. "If I give myself up to the magician for fifteen years I shall lose Zinaida. If I do not give myself up, I shall still lose her. It was the magician who found her for me. If only I could have one talk with her! But no, that would be useless. It would be impossible to explain the magician to Zinaida. All this would frighten her. For all her complexity she is very elementary. She would say that I must do what she advised; that is, live like other people, get a job somewhere, or something of that sort. This I cannot do; it is useless for me to try.

"But perhaps I am wrong about Zinaida again; perhaps she can understand everything, even the magician. It is true she said all that about life and ordinary circumstances, but it was from a different point of view and I never tried to explain things fully to her, though she always wanted me to tell her everything.

"But how strange it all is! Last night everything was over. I believed that Zinaida was going to be married; and I went to the magician and asked him to send me back so that I could change my life and put everything right. Then, while I was speaking to him, I suddenly realized that I had already come to him asking the same thing before and he had sent me back and I had found myself at school, and everything had gone the same way as before. Again I had done the same absurd things down to the smallest details, although I always knew beforehand what would happen. And again I came back to the magician.

"Can all this be really true? Perhaps none of it happened. Perhaps the magician simply put me to sleep and I dreamed that I was living my life over again. What actually happened? It is impossible to verify. I don't know and never shall know. Perhaps the truth lies in the very fact that it can neither be proved nor disproved.

"After all there is a difference. Yesterday I thought that Zinaida was going to be married: now I know that she could not have married Minsky. And now I have to decide what answer to give the magician. This is new. This did not happen before. And then, about the devil, what did he say about this disagreeable gentleman with horns and hoofs? There was something very interesting about it, but I must confess that I did not listen properly when he was speaking. I must ask him next time.

"Now the idea is that I must do something to prevent things from happening to me in the same way again. The magician said that in some way the devil is mixed up in this. How funny! I always thought that we could do our worst without any help from the devil . . . So the only thing to do is to give myself up to the magician. Strange! I have heard of such things before, but they always seemed to me to be invented and I saw no meaning or purpose in them. Now it appears that they actually happen and that there is much meaning in them and a very definite purpose. I know it is silly, but there is something in me that is a little afraid of the magician although at the same time I know that I am in a privileged position. I have nothing to be afraid of because I have nothing to lose and things cannot be worse than they are now."

Osokin slips his hand into his pocket and touches something cold and heavy. The revolver! He had quite forgotten it. He smiles ironically.

"Yes, the three roads of the Russian fairy tale," he says to himself. "If you take the first road you will lose your horse; if you take the second, you will perish yourself; and if you take the third, you will both lose your horse and perish yourself. Which to choose?"

He gets up and walks slowly along the boulevard.

Dawn is breaking.

"To-morrow I must give my answer. I cannot wait longer—though what answer I shall give I don't yet know. It is hard to believe that I can actually do nothing at all. But, at the same time, what have I done so far? I have only spoiled everything. To give myself up to the magician? That again seems strange, even cowardly. Probably this is where the greatest illusion lies, because to become convinced and to admit to oneself that one can actually do nothing is not cowardly at all. On the contrary, if it is true, this is the bravest thing one can do—but it is so difficult to believe. If only I could see Zinaida just once before I give my answer. He told me to take my time. Perhaps I can go to the Crimea. Things can always be arranged . . . Well, to-morrow!"

Osokin walks home.

Moscow is waking up. Church bells ring for early mass. Carriages rattle along. Dvorniks sweep the cobbled streets, raising clouds of dust. Two cats, one grey and white and the other yellow, sit opposite each other on the pavement, very intently, and seem to converse.

Osokin looks round, and suddenly an extraordinarily vivid sensation sweeps over him that, if he were not there, everything would be exactly the same.

FOR THE BEST IN PAPERBACKS, LOOK FOR THE 🐧

In every corner of the world, on every subject under the sun, Penguin represents quality and variety – the very best in publishing today.

For complete information about books available from Penguin – including Pelicans, Puffins, Peregrines and Penguin Classics – and how to order them, write to us at the appropriate address below. Please note that for copyright reasons the selection of books varies from country to country.

In the United Kingdom: Please write to *Dept E.P., Penguin Books Ltd, Harmondsworth, Middlesex, UB7 0DA*

If you have any difficulty in obtaining a title, please send your order with the correct money, plus ten per cent for postage and packaging, to *PO Box No 11, West Drayton, Middlesex*

In the United States: Please write to *Dept BA, Penguin, 299 Murray Hill Parkway, East Rutherford, New Jersey 07073*

In Canada: Please write to *Penguin Books Canada Ltd, 2801 John Street, Markham, Ontario L3R 1B4*

In Australia: Please write to the *Marketing Department, Penguin Books Australia Ltd, P.O. Box 257, Ringwood, Victoria 3134*

In New Zealand: Please write to the *Marketing Department, Penguin Books (NZ) Ltd, Private Bag, Takapuna, Auckland 9*

In India: Please write to *Penguin Overseas Ltd, 706 Eros Apartments, 56 Nehru Place, New Delhi, 110019*

In Holland: Please write to *Penguin Books Nederland B.V., Postbus 195, NL–1380AD Weesp, Netherlands*

In Germany: Please write to *Penguin Books Ltd, Friedrichstrasse 10–12, D–6000 Frankfurt Main 1, Federal Republic of Germany*

In Spain: Please write to *Longman Penguin España, Calle San Nicolas 15, E–28013 Madrid, Spain*

In France: Please write to *Penguin Books Ltd, 39 Rue de Montmorency, F-75003, Paris, France*

In Japan: Please write to *Longman Penguin Japan Co Ltd, Yamaguchi Building, 2–12–9 Kanda Jimbocho, Chiyoda-Ku, Tokyo 101, Japan*

ARKANA – NEW-AGE BOOKS FOR MIND, BODY AND SPIRIT

By the same author

A Further Record Extracts from Meetings 1928–1945

Originally published in a limited edition of just twenty copies, *A Further Record* encompasses the breadth of Ouspensky's teaching on a wide range of topics.

During the period 1928–45 Ouspensky held many meetings at which he gave detailed answers to his students' questions – whether those questions were naive or profound. In so doing he imparted a wealth of knowledge and a clear exposition of the system he had devised. The material in this book consists of verbatim extracts from those meetings.

Ouspensky's ideas on the nature of man and the cosmos span all aspects of our existence. Here his ideas are grouped by subject for ease of reference, with sections on self-remembering (including the nature and purpose of suffering), will, negative emotions, energy centres in man, cosmology, and the Lord's prayer.

ARKANA – NEW-AGE BOOKS FOR MIND, BODY AND SPIRIT

By the same author

In Search of the Miraculous Fragments
of an Unknown Teaching

Undoubtedly a *tour de force*. To put entirely new and very complex cosmology and psychology into fewer than 400 pages, and to do this with a simplicity and vividness that makes the book accessible to any educated reader, is in itself something of an achievement'
– *The Times Literary Supplement*

Probably his best-known work, Ouspensky's vivid account of his three years with G. I. Gurdjieff from 1915–18, working under the difficult conditions of war and revolution, is written with characteristic honesty.

The book describes Gurdjieff's cosmology from Ouspensky's own perspective as a student, and shows how Ouspensky's formulation of his own ideas eventually led to his break with Gurdjieff. It conveys a strong and lasting impression that not only did Ouspensky discover true knowledge about Man and his relationship with the Universe, but that a practical cosmic teaching for the conduct of life is even now in existence.

ARKANA – NEW-AGE BOOKS FOR MIND, BODY AND SPIRIT

By the same author

A New Model of the Universe

Ouspensky's third book considers a vast range of topics whose common theme is the nature and meaning of man's existence.

On an essentially religious level, Ouspensky examines the ways to study the New Testament and includes his thoughts on Esotericism, the problem of Superman, the symbolism of the Tarot and the systems of Yoga. He goes on to explore the recent ideas of the New Physics: relativity, problems of space and time, three-dimensional time, the fifth and sixth dimensions, and his own model of the universe.

Greatly influenced by the work of contemporary psychologists, he presents a study of dreams and describes the human mind in higher states of consciousness – an analysis that leads to an examination of clairvoyance. Other topics discussed include great monuments of religious or historical significance, a theory of time, and sex in relation to the evolution of man towards Superman. Above all, the impressive scope and depth of this remarkable book confirm Ouspensky's stature as one of the great thinkers of the twentieth century.

By the same author

Talks with a Devil

Talks with a Devil was written at around the same time as *A New Model of the Universe*, during the time that Ouspensky was searching and before he met Gurdjieff. It comprises two stories – *The Inventor* and *The Benevolent Devil* – dealing with two issues that concerned Ouspensky deeply. The first is that of conscious evil and the second the price one pays for 'good' behaviour.

An Introduction by J. G. Bennett places the tales in the context of Ouspensky's life and philosophy, and explores their connection with the Slavic folkloric tradition of demons and devils.